CATHERINE

THE COUSINS OF PEMBERLEY: BOOK 2

LINDA O'BYRNE

First Published by SpellBound Books 2022

PRINT ISBN:978-1-7396852-3-2

This book is dedicated to my nieces, Kerri and Karen.

You make my world brighter.

ALSO BY LINDA O'BYRNE

THE COUSINS OF PEMBERLEY:

BOOK I:

CASSANDRA

1

DERBYSHIRE, ENGLAND. 1833

It is a truth universally acknowledged, that when two young people meet, fall in love and become engaged, then it is only a matter of time before a wedding takes place. If there are no objections and no financial difficulties, then this marriage can happen quite speedily.

Sadly, in the case of Miss Cassandra Bennet and Dr Richard Courtney, two factors had delayed their longed-for ceremony. Cassandra, being related to the Darcys of Pemberley, had been thrilled when her Aunt Elizabeth announced that she would take charge of all the arrangements.

"With your own mother living away up in Newcastle, it is not practical, Cassandra, for her to be directly involved in all the decisions, although I know, of course, that she longs to play her part," Mrs Darcy had said tactfully, not wanting to make it too obvious that Lydia was refusing to pay a penny towards the bridal clothes or bridal breakfast. The tone had been set when she hadn't insisted that her daughter return home to be married.

Since the news had broken that her own scandalous marriage to George Wickham had been invalid and that Cassandra was therefore illegitimate, Lydia had stepped back from her role as mother of the bride and all the glory that went with that title. Reluctantly she had agreed to attend the wedding but, luckily for Cassandra and the Darcys, her husband, Colonel Allerton, had been sent to France with his regiment. His glowering presence would not be missed.

Cassandra, still in the joyous bliss of the newly engaged, agreed almost absentmindedly. She just wanted to marry her dear Richard and didn't really care who or what was arranged for the day. But then fate stepped in - twice. The Darcys had already planned a coming out ball for their twin daughters who were turning eighteen, a grand affair to be held at Matlock House, their London home, at Christmas. It just wasn't possible to plan a wedding so close to that grand occasion and so the middle of January had been agreed on by all as the next very suitable date.

Then, out of the blue, on the 10th of January, 1833, fate struck again, this time in a most unhappy way. Sir Edgar Courtney, Richard's father, who had been ill for some time, died and the wedding had to be postponed. Richard and his sister, Susannah, who kept house for him were summoned north to the county of Northumberland to help their brothers with all the sad arrangements for a funeral and it was felt only fitting that late March would now be the right time for the postponed marriage to take place.

Pemberley at any time of the year was a magnificent sight but many thought that in early Spring it was at its best - lambs on the hills, green leaves breaking, daffodils and late crocii studding the gardens with purple, white and gold.

The great house had been cleaned from cellar to attics, its many tall windows polished to brilliance, ready for the influx of visitors from all over the country. The actual wedding would, of course, be held in the local church but there was to be a grand luncheon reception back at Pemberley and dancing in the evening.

The housekeeper, Miss Reynolds, relation to the elderly lady who had once greeted a certain Miss Elizabeth Bennet and her uncle and aunt on a memorable visit many years ago, was so busy that she was beginning to wish she had never heard the word "wedding".

Finding accommodation for all the relations who were attending the ceremony was not difficult, because the one thing Pemberley did not lack was bedrooms. But making sure that Richard Courtney's elderly aunt and Mrs Darcy's own mother, Mrs Bennet and her sister, Mrs Collins had chambers of equal luxury and status had proved more of a headache.

Mrs Collins, in particular, was very alert both as to the situation of her room - the first had been declined as "too sunny", the second as "too high up" - and her position at the dining-table - she was not seated close enough to Elizabeth. Mrs Bennet had already complained that the flowers decorating her room were not as splendid as those she had spied elsewhere.

The rest of the staff were suffering from a frenzy of cleaning and, as Grace, one of the maids said tartly in the servants' hall as she tried to rest her aching legs, "if this is for a cousin of Pemberley, Lord help us when one of the Darcy daughters gets married."

To all this Cassandra and Richard were happily oblivious and if they lay awake the night before the ceremony, it was not from an excess of hard work.

Just as the sun was breaking over the hills on the day of the wedding, a young woman, small, thin, brown eyed, her brown hair flying free over her shoulders, with a shabby old cloak flung over her plain day dress, slipped from a side door and ran down the path, between the fine arrangements of spring flowers that lined each side, down the steps that lead through the rose garden, where the bushes were still sleeping, into the flower gardens beyond.

Catherine Collins had arrived the afternoon before with her step-mother, Kitty, her half-sister, Harriet, and Mrs Bennet. In all the flurry of unpacking, taking tea, greeting aunts and cousins, showing Harriet off to everyone and then making sure that the child had her bread and milk before she went to bed, Catherine had had no time at all to explore.

She had been forced to sit beside Harriet's bed for a long time - the little girl was too excited to sleep and so even investigating the wonderful house had been postponed. But this morning Harriet was still fast asleep and Grace, one of the Pemberley maids was on reluctant duty in the nursery. She had told Catherine, almost impudently, that she was a lady's maid and made it quite clear by her attitude that she was annoyed at being told to take care of Harriet for a little while, but Miss Reynolds, the housekeeper, had insisted.

Mrs Bennet and Kitty Collins were still in their rooms, so Catherine had taken the chance to explore outside where no one could find her.

Being on her own, doing exactly what she wanted was such a rare occurrence that it went to her head like strong wine. Her whole life was governed by cries of "Catherine! Where are you? Catherine, bring me this, do that..." There was never any time to stop and think, to be just herself. Now she gulped in deep breaths of the clear, pure Derbyshire air, wondering why it tasted so different from that in Hertfordshire.

The glorious woods were too far to reach this morning because she knew she could not be away from her duties to her sister for long, but she idled her way through the gardens, enjoying the arbours and statuary, the spring flowers and the new leaves bursting into life and hearing in the distance the cries of the sheep and their lambs up on the hillsides.

"I do wish Papa could see these gardens," she murmured to herself. Sadly, she was well aware that Mr Collins was not and never would be a sensible man. He was pompous and some of the things he said in public and even from the pulpit of his church, made her wince and bite her tongue in shame. That the Darcys had no time for him was quite apparent from various remarks she had overheard, including her stepmother declaring to her older sister on their arrival that it was wonderful to be away from William for a short while!

But for all his faults, Catherine loved him: they shared an interest in nature and growing things, although whilst she found comfort in the beauty of flowers and trees, her papa preferred growing cabbages and lettuces. Catherine knew he would have enjoyed these wonderful gardens and was sad that his duties in the church living of Meryton prevented him from travelling north with the rest of his family.

"Oh, how pretty!" She had rounded a bend in the path and found it led to a small glade of trees where the woods began, clustered around a fish pond - a stone fountain splashed and played, fed by a stream that flowed through the grounds from the hills on its way to one of the many Pemberley lakes.

Thick green turf ran round the outside of the stone basin and, without a second thought, Catherine shook off her shoes and felt the soft damp grass under her feet. It was a glorious feeling of freedom as the light breeze rustled the branches and her hair, swept back in profusion, showed the chestnut and bronze glints that normally never showed under her severe braided style. She swayed gently to a tune in her head, then humming, danced a few little steps in time to the splashing of the water.

She wondered what it would be like to live with all this beauty around her, every day. Her home at Longbourn was very pleasant with a garden and orchard and a pretty wilderness alongside the driveway, but nothing compared to the grounds of Pemberley.

As she paced a few dance steps in the sunlight that was now piercing the leaves above her head, she chided herself. She was lucky to have been included in the wedding party. Cassandra was only a very distant cousin, indeed Mrs Darcy, her godmother, was a closer relation to Catherine: it was indeed kind of them to invite her.

It was difficult not to be aware of where you stood in a large family with so many different branches, hard not to realise that you were a very small, insignificant twig on one of those branches. Catherine had no high expectations of the years in front of her. If she did in fact marry - and common-sense told her that she probably would - the man in question would be one of her father's junior clergymen who needed a wife and helpmate in his living.

Sadly, unless they came from rich families, young men just starting their careers in the church usually found themselves working in the poorest parts of towns and cities, not in beautiful countryside. Catherine could even have accepted that situation, been happy to have lived in genteel poverty if she had ever met a gentleman who appealed to her as a husband. Sadly, the junior clergy who had come to her attention so far had not inclined her to give up her spinster state!

She wished her grandparents, Sir William Lucas and his wife were still alive. They had, according to Mama Collins, often held grand parties with plenty of partners to choose from. But they had both passed away and her Aunt Maria had married a farmer and moved to distant Cornwall.

Yes, Catherine was well aware that her future was either a marriage of convenience or staying at home as unpaid nursery maid to her small half-sister. Living with a step-mother who spent most of her time complaining about her life had made Catherine determined that she would not succumb to groaning and grouching. It served no purpose and only annoyed everyone who heard.

She had long ago determined to be sanguine and resolute in facing these problems but deliberately buried under a heavy cloak of common-sense and staid manners, was a character that was at complete odds with her outward demeanour. It was this joy of living, a love of fun and laughter that now broke through on this glorious Spring day.

Sir Robert Courtney was not a happy man. Rising before dawn, he'd left Pemberley, striding out of the grounds and into the woods. He hadn't slept well, tossing and turning, his mind full of his new responsibilities as the owner of Courtney Castle and the surrounding Northumberland estate. He was impatient for this wedding of his younger brother to be over. He was fond of Richard and liked the girl, wishing them both well, but time spent away from home was always a problem for him.

His father had been ill for many years and, refusing to take advice from his son, the estate had fallen into disrepair. Sir Robert knew that with hard work and money, it would flourish again, but although the hard work was not a problem, the money was. What he needed was a rich wife, but....

As ever he tried to put Lucinda, the wife who had died so tragically, out of his mind but it wasn't easy. He knew his family wanted him to marry again and produce a male heir. The inheritance of the Courtney estate was passed down through the male line.

This especially horrified his other brother, Martin, who was next in line to inherit, an event that filled that young man with terror! His indolent life style mostly spent in the gaming houses of London and on the country's various race-tracks, did not countenance the responsibilities such a change in style would bring about and Robert knew that within a year his brother would have run through all the money that the estate made and plunge the Courtneys into dreadful debt.

But marrying again filled Robert with despair. He had cared for Lucinda and had been deeply moved when she died in a coaching accident two years past. She had been so beautiful - with golden hair, tall and slim, accomplished in painting and music and with an oddly remote air that he had found intriguing. He had known her since they were children and had grown up determined that they would marry. How could he replace her in his life? Anyone else would be but a mere shadow. Except - and this was the point he came up against every time in his musings - there was Matilda.

His daughter was six years old now with the same fair loveliness which had adorned her mother. Matilda had been inside the phaeton with Lucinda when it had overturned on a steep slope outside Whitby. But somehow she had escaped unscathed, except that from that day on, she had never spoken. The child was intelligent, he knew that, and he blamed himself for not taking more time and trouble to reverse her affliction. He had been remiss to leave her in the hands of her nurse for the past two years but, every time he looked at her, he saw Lucinda and the pain of her death returned.

The only other member of the family who lived in Courtney Castle was his very elderly Aunt Honoria, who at this very moment was probably intimidating the other guests at Pemberley. She was a strict disciplinarian and he feared that Matilda was scared of her. No, his daughter needed a governess or, at the very least, a sensible, intelligent companion who could try and help her learn so that she could play some role in the life ahead of her.

Well, that was one decision made. He resolved to find a suitable young woman as soon as he could and resolved to ask Elizabeth Darcy for her help. She had a wide range of acquaintances; surely amongst them would be just the type of person he was looking for?

This break away from home had clarified his mind about marriage as well. He had experienced love and could see from Richard's demeanor towards Cassandra that it was an enviable state, but this time he would marry for duty. He would not let his heart become involved.

"Abigail Richmond will accept my proposal," he muttered now as he made his way back towards Pemberley along a narrow woodland track. "She does not love me and I do not love her, but it will be a sensible union for both of us. We have known each other since childhood, she was a great friend of Lucinda's, she is good-looking, well-bred and wealthy and if she brings me an heir, then all well and good."

Coming to a conclusion, he stopped to take a deep breath and then frowned. He could have sworn he heard singing. He followed the sound and from the shelter of the bushes he looked out to where a small glade had been cut into the woods and a pretty fountain played into a pool. And he smiled.

There, in front of him, was a girl, no doubt by her dress and appearance, one of the Pemberley maids, dancing on the grass, her bare feet wet with the spray from the fountain. Her beautiful long brown hair was swinging loose and with arms outstretched she was singing softly to herself, lost in a happy world of feeling and music.

For a moment the black clouds that seemed to surround him every day lifted, and he recalled how happiness had once felt. He was well aware that knowing he would one day inherit Courtney Castle had placed a sense of responsibility on his shoulders from a very young age. As he'd grown, the occasions in life when he could relax and have fun had grown fewer and fewer and with Lucinda's death had vanished altogether.

He was about to step back and leave her to her solitude when the sound of clapping broke out. There, on the other side of the glade, stood his brother Martin, laughing down at the girl who gave a gasp and pulled her cloak firmly round her shoulders.

"Sir! You startled me!" Catherine was mortified to find someone watching her being silly. The young man was very good-looking; tall and slim, elegantly dressed, with sparkling green eyes and a wicked smile.

He swept off his hat with a flourish, one lock of bright gold falling over his forehead. "A thousand apologies, little fairy girl. But do continue with your dance or will you vanish into thin air now someone has spied you?"

Catherine felt her cheeks flush. "Sir, you must give me leave to retire to the house."

Martin Courtney took a long stride forward and reached out to stop her as she backed away. This was the most fun he had had since arriving at Pemberley for Richard's wedding.

He had been only too happy to leave London - and all the debts that he seemed to have incurred in such a short time. He knew he would have to have one of those boring conversations with his older brother before the day was out. He needed money and Robert would lecture and lecture - lord how strict and old-fashioned he had become since his wife died!

Although he found that exceedingly irritating, there was also something sad about his brother's situation. Martin could still remember a brother who had been ready for any adventure. For sure he had always known that he was heir to Courtney and apparently enjoyed working to enhance the family's fortunes, but he had still had a light-hearted side to his nature.

He'd looked forward to meeting Cassandra, whom he had found beautiful but so in love with his younger brother that she had hardly looked in his direction once. The two older Darcy girls were too well mannered to flirt.

There was, of course, the youngest Darcy daughter, Bennetta, whose dark curls he found captivating, but she was not yet seventeen, admittedly old enough to marry but he could tell she was still a child in so many ways! He had to admit that flirting with her was a dangerous prospect, like playing with fire, even though her dark eyes had sparkled and gleamed mischievously in his direction. There was no way he wanted to incur the wrath of Mr Fitzwilliam Darcy by becoming entangled with his youngest daughter. At least not for a couple of years! This maid, dancing to a tune she alone could hear, was the only other girl he had met who quickened his interest.

"Why, are you late beginning your daily duties? I am one of the Darcys' guests. Isn't it your duty to serve me?"

Catherine pulled the hood of her cloak up over her head. She hesitated; the man had obviously mistaken her for a servant but even so he should not talk to her in that intimate way. She knew that she should just tell him who she was and ask him to escort her back to the house, but a sudden most unexpected spurt of anger at his attitude kept her quiet. Let him be embarrassed when they met at the wedding later that day. She had done nothing to be ashamed about. She turned to go and the man reached out with a laugh and caught hold of her arm.

"Let her go!"

They both swung round as a tall, dark haired man with broad shoulders, pushed aside a tangle of over-hanging branches and strode into the glade.

"You are up and about early." The younger man turned to him as he spoke and released her with a smile.

The man glared at him and at Catherine. "I think it best if you return to your duties, Miss," he snapped and she thought she could see cold contempt in his deep blue eyes. "Dallying in the woods is not a sensible course of action for a young woman." He glared at the younger man, "And lord knows why you would wish to annoy Darcy by making free with his servants."

Catherine didn't know whether to laugh or cry. Dallying! When had she ever done that? She didn't even know how to dally.

The fair haired man had let go of her arm and was smiling at her. "I suppose you are right. Yes, pretty maid, as tempting as you are, off you go, back to the house."

With a brief curtsey to them both, Catherine turned and hurried away.

"Stop!"

She turned, flustered, to find the dark haired man standing behind her. Without a word he thrust her shoes into her hands and she knew he was still watching as she took them and fled barefoot back down the path towards the house.

Elizabeth Darcy stood at a window of Pemberley, gazing out over the grounds to where the woodlands gave way to the Derbyshire hills: she never tired of this view that calmed her spirits and gave her joy. She felt exhausted; the wedding had been the day before and everything had gone well. The happy couple had left to spend a week in a small manor house that Mr Darcy owned just outside of Stratford upon Avon.

"You are tired, Elizabeth. You have done too much as usual. Why will you never learn to delegate to the staff? Miss Reynolds is quite capable of managing all the arrangements." A warm hand placed on her shoulder, the voice in her ear of her beloved was all she needed to lean back, feeling his strength supporting her and all her cares drift away.

"No, not too much. Just enough. It is never the household concerns that are tiring, it is dealing with all the different members of our families and their various needs." She turned in his arms and then, realising he was wearing his riding clothes smiled and said, "I see you are escaping from the ritual 'after the wedding discussions', my dear. How very wise."

Mr Darcy shuddered. "I am rescuing Charles from the hell on earth of deciding whose hat was the most fetching, who danced with whom more than once and who will be the next in line to reach the altar. Sir Robert and the rest of the Courtney relations have already sent their thanks and left; they wanted to be on the road before dawn, as you know, so Charles and I will ride up onto the hills, exercise our horses and enjoy ourselves." He bent and kissed her fingers. "I will see you at dinner, but please do not seat me next to Lydia or Kitty if you value my sanity."

Elizabeth was still smiling at the dread in his voice as she made her way into the yellow drawing-room. She stopped in the doorway as she considered the occupants sitting on the sofas, drinking hot chocolate and eating little almond biscuits.

This was the first time the four sisters had been together alone for years and years. The only one missing was Mary, married to the Reverend Matthew Malliot, an elderly missionary. She led a very different life from her sisters, preaching to the people of Africa. Elizabeth always felt sorry for those poor people. Listening to Mary's diatribes all day must be very wearying.

"La, Lizzie, do come and sit down. The chocolate's getting cold." Lydia had put her feet up on the sofa and Elizabeth could see a great deal of green stocking and the snags her shoes were making on the silk covering.

"Yes, I'm sure you have enough servants to run this vast place without you always having to interfere."

Kitty sounded irritated, dissatisfied. Ever since she had married William Collins, following the death of his wife Charlotte, she had realised that her life style would never be as high as that of her two elder sisters.

The present Mrs Collins had hoped that when Sir William Lucas and his wife passed away, that their granddaughter, Catherine, would have inherited a tidy sum and therefore contribute greatly to the Collins' annual expenditure. But it had transpired that Sir William had made many foolish investments in the city and the knowledge of his wealth was based on nothing but rumours. Catherine had inherited nothing.

Sighing, she ate another biscuit: Kitty had found that food was an enormous comfort when your husband was a pompous fool - as her daily increasing girth showed only too well.

"Lizzie, you look tired. I'm sure you should be - it was a wonderful occasion yesterday. Cassandra looked lovely. You must be proud of her, Lydia."

Elizabeth took her seat next to Jane Bingley and cast her an anxious glance. She was very pale which only emphasized the beauty of her face. A few months before she had given birth to her fourth child, a little girl they had named Alethea. This very late and unexpected arrival seemed to have drained her health and vitality.

"Oh lord, yes, I am proud, of course I am. I must admit she looked very pretty but then wearing that dress and that wonderful emerald necklace, so would any girl. Yours, I take it, Lizzie?"

Lydia had watched her daughter's wedding with mixed emotions. It had brought back memories of her own marriage to George Wickham, a marriage she now knew to have been a complete sham. She recalled the vast, cold, empty church in London, the grim faces of her aunt and uncle and Mr Darcy. And there had definitely been no emerald necklace for her to wear on her special day! But she comforted herself with the knowledge that both grooms at her weddings, firstly to Wickham and then to dear Major Allerton, had looked far smarter and more handsome in their uniforms than the thin, dark-haired doctor that Cassandra had married.

Elizabeth nodded and poured herself a cup of chocolate. "The necklace? Indeed. Weddings are such fun and I have no idea when I will get a chance to dress another bride. The twins have no beaux at present and Bennetta's choice is likely to be a pirate or a highwayman!"

Jane smiled. "My Beth will be eighteen soon and so I suppose I shall have to start thinking of what young man she will bring into the family."

"At present all our daughters are closeted in the twins' bedroom, refurbishing their bonnets for church on Sunday. And gossiping as we are, I have no doubt, about Cassandra's wedding." She glanced round the room. "But we are short of the family gathering. Where is Mama and I noticed that Catherine was not with the other girls?"

Kitty popped another biscuit into her mouth. "Mama is lying down, having an attack of nervous exhaustion from the wedding party. Catherine is looking after Harriet, of course."

"But Kitty, you were given a nursery maid for the child when you arrived. It is surely not Catherine's place to take care of her little sister all the time. She should be relaxing with her cousins."

"Oh, she enjoys it. She adores Harriet."

"But - "

"Oh don't fuss so, Lizzie. Come and sit down and tell us who was the very old lady with that ridiculously large purple hat who sat right in front at the church? One of Richard's relations, I suppose. I do declare I could hardly listen to the ceremony for laughing."

Lydia and Jane chimed in with their comments and Elizabeth sat back, strangely dissatisfied. Catherine Collins was not a nursery maid, whatever her stepmother might think.

The following day found Mr and Mrs Darcy standing on the entrance steps of Pemberley, waving as two carriages made their way down the drive. "Well, my dear, there go the Bingleys with all their children and, to my lasting delight they have taken your mother and Lydia with them. When was that arranged?"

"Last night. Jane, whom I believe to be a saint in human form, told Mama that she needed her advice about some refurbishments she was planning for the house and Lydia decided that she will stay with the Bingleys until she makes her way north once more. I think she is going to try and persuade Charles to give her some money and I expect she will be successful. Charles is a dear soul but has no defences against Lydia's wheedling and Jane is just as soft-hearted."

"Did it seem strange to have your sisters together under the same roof?"

"Indeed it did. We sat yesterday, talking and squabbling and apart from Mary not being there to add her caustic comments, twenty or so years might not have passed!"

"Come and sit down. I will ring for coffee."

Elizabeth smiled as they made their way down the main staircase and crossed the vast black and white squared hall towards the stairs that led up towards the next floor where the yellow drawing-room was situated - one of her favourite places to relax.

"You forget that we still have a house full of guests to entertain."

A sudden screeching rang out and Mr Darcy flinched. "And that is the noisiest, I do believe."

There was another screech and a small girl of about four came running from the passageway that led to the servants' side of the house, clutching a piece of bread and jam in her hand. She skidded to a halt in front of the Darcys and peered up at them through a tangle of curls, then pushed the wedge of bread into a mouth that was already far too full, as if she was determined no one should take her prize away from her.

"Harriet Collins - what are you doing down here?" Mrs Darcy said, exasperated.

Just then, footsteps sounded and a small, thin young woman in a plain brown dress, her hair braided up around her head, came running into the hall. "Oh Harriet - there you are! Naughty girl. I have been searching for you everywhere. What are you eating - oh, you have jam all over your nice clean dress."

"Catherine, my dear."

"Mrs Darcy, Mr Darcy!" The girl dropped them a curtsey and then bent, trying to wipe jam off the wriggling and squirming child with her handkerchief.

"Catherine, we have discussed this before. There is no need for you to be so correct. Please call me Cousin Elizabeth. I am your godmother and your second cousin."

The girl's face blushed pink. "Yes, I forgot. I'm just so pleased to have found Harriet. Mama Collins has been asking for her for the past hour and she was nowhere in sight."

Mr Darcy turned away from them with a curt bow. "My dear, I will leave you to these domestic problems and will see you at dinner."

Elizabeth watched him go then, with a frown, turned back to Catherine who was struggling to stop the little girl from running off once more. "I don't understand why you are in charge of your sister again. Where is her nursery maid? I know one was allocated to her when you all arrived for the wedding as Kitty had not seen fit to bring one with her."

"Harriet - stand still and mind your manners. Your aunt is speaking. I am sorry, Cousin Elizabeth. Mama Collins prefers me to look after her. I do at home, you know, and Mama Collins thinks it is better if her little world is not disturbed by too much change. She is a very sensitive child."

Elizabeth stared down with distaste at Harriet now standing, scowling at the floor, still munching on a huge mouthful of bread and jam. She was as tall as she was wide and although in Elizabeth's opinion all children were attractive in their different ways, this child of Kitty and Mr Collins sometimes made her think perhaps she was wrong in this view. And if this child was sensitive, then the moon was made from cheese.

"Obviously Kitty knows her daughter best, but you look tired, my dear." Swiftly she rang a small handbell sitting on a console table and when a footman appeared, she told him to take Miss Harriet to her mother immediately and if Mrs Collins queried him, he was to say that was Mrs Darcy's orders.

When Harriet had been removed, she linked arms with Catherine and walked her upstairs into the drawing-room. "I was about to ring for coffee. Will you join me? We have had little time to talk since you arrived."

Catherine sat and gazed around the luxurious room with its dark yellow drapes and furnishings. She felt anxious: it was all very well Cousin Elizabeth telling her sister what to do, but she knew Mama Collins would be very angry that she had somehow allowed Harriet to run off and ruin her luncheon with bread and jam.

"Did you enjoy the wedding?"

"Oh, what I saw of it was wonderful," Catherine replied swiftly. "Cassandra looked lovely and so happy and Dr Courtney is a very handsome man, but sadly Harriet began to cry - she wanted to play with the flowers at the end of the pew - so I had to take her out of the church and missed some of the ceremony."

Elizabeth bit her lip. She had certainly heard a child shrieking at some point, but it had quickly stopped and she hadn't given it another thought. Just then another memory surfaced. "And the evening celebrations? I don't think I saw you dancing, but there was such a crowd that I might not have noticed."

Catherine folded her hands in her lap. This was so difficult; it made it sound as if she was ungrateful for the invitation to Cassandra's wedding. "Harriet wouldn't settle. Sadly she found her way to the kitchen and the servants plied her with cake and sweets. So she was a trifle ill and Mama Collins thought it best if I stayed with her."

Just then a footman brought in a pot of coffee on a silver tray and Elizabeth dismissed him, serving them herself, She watched as Catherine sipped. Such a calm young woman, composed and obviously full of the same down-to-earth common-sense that had governed her mother, Charlotte, and led to her marrying William Collins so many years ago. But there was also a wistful expression in her eyes that was worrisome to Elizabeth.

"Do you miss your mama?" she asked eventually.

Catherine flushed. "Of course, I do! She was so gentle and kind and tried to help people. I try to be like her, but I'm afraid I will never succeed."

"You are over twenty now, of course. Do you think of marriage yet. Do you have many beaux at home?"

Catherine shook her head. "Mama Collins often complains at the lack of eligible young men in the district, especially since the militia has left town. But she also says that she cannot do without me at present in helping to care for Harriet. Mama Collins is sure that in a few years' time, when Harriet is older, I will make a match with one of the young clergymen Papa knows."

Her voice trailed away as she realised she was finding it difficult to sound enthusiastic at the prospect ahead of her.

"And does that satisfy you, my dear? Looking after your little sister? I loved your mama, as you know. We were good friends for years. I am sure that the life of a nursery maid is not one she would have chosen for you."

"Oh, I love Harriet, indeed I do, but sometimes I long to see more of the world."

For a second the sensible Catherine vanished and, to her surprise, Elizabeth caught a glimpse of a very different girl. "This is my first trip away from Hertfordshire since we moved there from Kent. I yearn to travel, to see different beautiful places. I would love to see the sea, to watch waves breaking on a beach. It is always described so beautifully in books. And do you know, I have never even been to London?"

"Well, that is a shame, although we have a house in London, I must admit I prefer the countryside. Still, you never know what life holds in store for you." She smiled at her god-daughter. "If I recall correctly your education is far superior to that of mine or my sisters."

Catherine hesitated; she felt that talking of her accomplishments seemed like boasting.

"Lady Catherine de Bourgh, Mr Darcy's aunt, whom I am named after, of course, although she was not my godmother, took a great interest in me when I was a small child and we were living near the great house of Rosings. She insisted that I had lessons in French and other useful subjects, gave me leave to use the Rosings' library and even kindly suggested books that I should read to improve my mind. Her daughter, Miss Anne, taught me to play the piano a little and I enjoy painting and sketching when I get the chance. But that isn't very often. I love plants and flowers, as does my Papa. We enjoy our garden together."

Elizabeth raised an eyebrow. It was so peculiar to think of Mr Darcy's aunt doing something kind for a child who could have meant nothing to her. "That was good of Lady Catherine."

Her namesake smiled warmly. "Yes, it was. I liked her. I know she appeared harsh and intolerant to many people, but she always had a pleasant word for me and I never found her unjust."

Elizabeth found her lips twitching. Her own youngest daughter, Bennetta, had offended Lady Catherine so much when a child that she had refused to visit Pemberley for over a year. What was it about this small, slim person that had touched the heart of a dragon? What had the old lady seen that others had not?

"I am well pleased to hear it. Now, if you have finished your coffee, I suggest you go and find one of my daughters and ask them to walk in the gardens with you to get some roses into your cheeks."

She sat thinking after Catherine left the room, recalling a long conversation she had recently had with Sir Robert Courtney. He was looking for a kind, sensible, intelligent girl, trustworthy and biddable, to be a companion to his young daughter in their castle on the Northumberland coast. Elizabeth Darcy thought she might know just the right person, someone who was, indeed, longing to see the ocean.

2

Catherine sat on the very edge of her seat in the pony trap, clutching a large parcel wrapped up in brown paper and string. Wooden hatches containing two clucking chickens and a dozen fluffy yellow chicks stood on the floor next to her and an enormous sack of potatoes was squashing her against the side of the trap.

Shivering, she was very cold, even though she was wearing her heavy dark blue skirt and jacket and a warm cloak. The wind that whistled in from the North Sea was bitter, even though the sun was shining in a pale blue sky.

She gasped and jolted forward as the little trap, the shaggy pony was pulling, hit a large bump in the uneven track. The young boy driving turned, laughed and told her to hold on tight in an accent she could only just understand.

Nodding, she wished her whole body didn't ache so much, longing for this journey to be over and only hoping that at the end there would be a bed she could fall into to sleep. But as tired as she was, she knew she was too excited to relax. The past few days had been such a whirlwind that her mind had found no time to settle down and let her think things through clearly and calmly.

Her whole life had been turned upside down in a matter of hours. Back at Pemberley, a week or so after the wedding, she'd realised that Cousin Elizabeth and Mama Collins had been closeted together for hours, but she had been so busy caring for Harriet that she hadn't had time to wonder what it was that they were talking about with the drawing-room door closed. Then to her astonishment she was called to Mama Collins' bedroom and found her over-seeing a maid packing her portmanteau.

"Are we leaving so soon? I thought we were to stay until the end of the week."

Mama Collins had glanced at her and said, almost as if it didn't matter. "Mama, Harriet and I are leaving tomorrow."

"Am I to stay? How will you manage with Harriet on the journey?"

"Really, Catherine, you make it sound as if you are indispensable. Not an attractive trait. No, of course you are not staying at Pemberley. What use would you be here? Apparently, Lizzie has been asked by Sir Robert Courtney to find a companion for his young daughter for a few months until he marries. She has written to him about you and received a favourable reply. They seem to think you would be suitable, goodness knows why, and so you are to travel north with Lydia as far as Newcastle and then you will journey on to Alnwick where you'll be met by one of the Courtney servants and taken further up the coast to Courtney Castle."

"But...."

"Please don't argue with me, Catherine! I have a dreadful headache. I am so fatigued. It is a good opportunity for you to be of use rather than just lazing around at home. You met Sir Robert at the wedding, did you not?"

Catherine had thought back to that day. She was sure she had never been introduced to Richard Courtney's eldest brother. She would have remembered.

"Anyways, it is all arranged. Lizzie always get her own way over these things but at least she has had the decency to realise that I am struggling at Longbourn with your father and my mother to care for, let alone Harriet. So she is sending a nursery maid and a house-maid to add to our staff."

Kitty Collins felt a great wave of satisfaction. Two extra servants - that would raise her status in the district and, what was even more important, the Darcys would continue to pay their annual wages which was a great comfort.

Catherine could get no more details from her stepmother and had vowed to speak to her Cousin Elizabeth as soon as she could. She had no desire at all to go north and look after another small girl.

But her plans were ruined when news came the next day that Mrs Jane Bingley had been taken ill. She had never fully recovered from the birth the year before of a baby who had arrived very late in life and Mrs Darcy had rushed from Pemberley to be at her sister's side. Aunt Lydia Allerton had returned from the Bingleys where she'd been staying and told Catherine to pack and be ready to set out the next day. And so there had been no chance to discuss anything with her cousin and she was too in awe of Mr Darcy to bring up with him what he would consider a very unimportant matter.

She had packed the few clothes she had brought with her for the wedding and wondered how she was going to manage in the north with such a sparcity of necessities. Luckily, Bennetta, whom she preferred out of all the Darcy cousins, had realised she was sadly under equipped for such a journey and that even a stay as long as three months would require more than two pairs of shoes, her travelling attire and three day dresses. She had given Catherine some thicker dresses and a warm cloak to keep out the wind, if not the rain.

The three Darcy girls were sitting on Catherine's bed, watching her pack. Miss Darcy, Anne, the elder twin, had offered nothing to help boost the meagre supply of clothing, but Jane had brought petticoats and stockings, neatly tied up with ribbon.

As Catherine thanked her, she wondered why everyone thought the two girls were identical. She glanced at them now in the mirror as she worked - both tall and fair and blue-eyed, but Anne had all the haughty demeanour of her father, which Catherine did not think sat well on her face. She was a girl who was always quite sure she was right in everything she did or thought.

Her sister, although her features and colouring were almost the same, was a gentle creature and the icy blue of her sister's gaze was a warm speedwell blue in hers as she helped Catherine fold garments to pack in her almost empty trunk.

"We girls have a whole different wardrobe for when we travel north to Scotland to stay with our Aunt Georgiana," she explained. "It gets colder and colder as you travel up the country, and even though you will be there during the summer, you will feel the difference."

"Being short of stature, like me, my garments will suit you best. I won't miss them," Bennetta said cheerfully. "Papa gives us a very generous dress allowance and when Mama returns from the Bingleys, she will quite understand what I have done and why."

She had picked up the dresses that Catherine had laid on the bed to pack and wrinkled up her nose. "Why are all your clothes grey or brown or dark horrid blue? Look - this one is not even a pretty pale grey, but a gloomy shade."

Catherine had felt herself blush. "I spend a lot of time with Harriet and all small children become so very sticky and dirty. Mama Collins thought it much more sensible if I had clothes that would not show every mark."

Bennetta had been going to say exactly what she thought of that, but then decided that wasn't wise. A few months previously she would have said just what she wanted, but she felt older and more sensible these days. Lord, was she growing elderly before her seventeenth birthday?

"Well, all my clothes are bright and cheerful. I love red and pink and yellow and white. You can't wear brown and grey all your life, Catherine! You aren't even twenty and three yet Lord, look - your dress for the evening is the dullest of mauves. You don't have the right colouring to wear mauve. It's for very old ladies, not young women!

Anne was beginning to feel indignant. "You will certainly need two good dresses for the evening as well as day clothes. I have no idea if Sir Robert entertains, or even if you would be invited to join his friends for dinner, but if you are, you need to look neat and respectable. You are not going north as a serving girl, Catherine. You are to be a companion and governess for just a few months, so I have been told. That is an entirely different thing."

Anne was always very keen that the social graces were meticulously observed. Catherine might be a very distant cousin, but she was still related to the Darcys of Pemberley and as such Anne was determined she should be treated with the respect the name commanded, whether Catherine deserved it or not!

"Indeed, you may well be sensible to speak to Miss Smith, who used to be our governess and is now a chaperone for when we need one," Jane said quietly. "I'm sure you met her at the wedding. She may have some old books you could use for your new charge from when we were children. I'm sure no one would miss them from our schoolroom. Our brothers are way past the age of being entertained by childish things."

"Were you not introduced to Sir Robert and his brother Mr Martin Courtney at the wedding, Catherine?" Anne was intrigued.

"And don't forget their dreadful aunt - she was the lady sitting at the very front in church wearing an enormous purple hat!" Bennetta laughed, hugging her knees to her chest.

Catherine shook her head. She didn't want to explain all over again about Harriet causing her to miss most of the ceremony and the dancing afterwards.

"I liked Mr Martin Courtney. He is probably the handsomest man I have ever met"

"Bennetta!" Jane sounded shocked. "He is the most dreadful flirt. I could see Papa frowning at him all evening."

"Papa frowns at any young man who looks at any of us twice. Woe betide one who looks a third time! I expect Papa would have them run out of the county. I don't know how he expects us ever to get married when he is determined to frighten away any man who shows even the slightest interest in us. I fear I shall be forced to elope and then he'll be sorry!"

Anne gazed at her reflection in the bedroom mirror and was pleased with what she saw. She knew that she would make a good marriage with someone of wealth and distinction. And, whatever her father said, she would marry the man she wanted. She was Miss Darcy of Pemberley and her only regret in life was that she had not been born a boy so she could inherit the estate. She was quite certain that she would do a far better job than Fitz would when he was older. All he cared about was his stupid books. It was so unfair that Pemberley would be his one day and she would have to watch him muddle his way through caring for it.

Jane sighed. If she were honest, she was a little scared of men. She never knew what to say to them and when she finally made up her mind, she realised that Anne had already spoken and the conversation had continued without her. Would she ever marry? Well, she was quite certain that would never happen until her twin sister became a bride.

Catherine, to whom marriage was not even a consideration, packed her borrowed possessions and wondered just what lay ahead of her.

A conversation with Miss Smith, the governess, did nothing to qualm her fears. A person of reduced circumstances, who had been only too pleased to find a home at Pemberley as governess to the Darcy girls, had now been given the onerous task of chaperone, as even Mrs Darcy had admitted it was futile trying to install any more knowledge into Bennetta's head.

"Dear girls, all three," Miss Smith had said as she sorted out a few rather battered books for Catherine to take north. "But one cannot say that the task is easy, Miss Collins. Indeed no. Spirited young ladies, with minds of their own, it is hard to make them concentrate and study and then, of course you are faced with explaining to their parents why they are not making better progress."

Catherine nodded; she could quite understand that. "But now you are their chaperone. A far easier job, I imagine."

Miss Smith, who already knew that her shortcomings in authority made her a less than adequate companion, especially for Miss Bennetta, tried to smile brightly, trying to forget that Mrs Darcy had already had words with her on that very subject. And if she lost this position at Pemberley, what would become of her?

"Oh yes, indeed. And, of course, you will only have one little girl to care for. I think, perhaps, I could have managed one with ease, but three! Anyway, I wish you joy of your task, indeed I do."

The journey from Derbyshire to Newcastle had seemed very long, made even longer by Lydia Allerton's lack of intelligent conversation. Catherine had nothing pertinent to say about the length of skirts this year or whether bonnets should be trimmed with black or red and so eventually the silences between them had grown longer and longer. She was quite certain that her distant cousin considered her a very dull girl and began to think that perhaps she was.

When they finally reached the large town of Newcastle, Lydia bade her goodbye and left her without a backwards glance. Catherine had spent the night at an inn, luckily sharing a room with two widowed ladies who were heading for Scotland. They had been horrified to discover she was travelling alone and at first had been suspicious of her character. But on hearing her story, they had relented and, in their company, she had taken the post carriage to Alnwick where a pony and trap waited for her. The young boy driving it had told her his name was Donald and her trunk was squeezed in amongst the boxes and bags of groceries.

As they left the town, the sight of Alnwick Castle had filled her with wonder. It was huge and awe-inspiring, seeming to fill the whole skyline, dominating the world around it.

"Oh what a magnificent sight! Can we not stop for a moment or two to explore?"

Donald had shook his dark curly head and shaken up the pony into a trot. "Nay, miss. I've been told not to waste any time on the road today." He had a very strong accent, one that Catherine had never heard before.

She gazed back over her shoulder. "Surely Courtney Castle cannot be that size?"

Her words were greeted with laughter. "Indeed no, miss. Courtney is just a tiddler, compared to Alnwick and Bamburgh. You'll see when we get there. We swing off towards the sea now and follow the coast north. Reckon you don't have castles like this down south."

Catherine knew that Windsor and Arundel were very big buildings, but Donald seemed so proud of his county's castles that she just shook her head and profoundly hoped that the boy was right and that Courtney Castle was a little more home-like.

She returned to gazing around her at the wild scenery, the soaring seabirds with their harsh cries overhead. Then suddenly she gave a cry and jumped to her feet before sitting down again with a jolt that knocked the breath from her body. They had rounded a bend in the road and there lay the great gleaming expanse of the sea.

Catherine had always longed to see an ocean. She had read so many books where it was described; the waves, the colour, the sound of surf on rocks. But the vastness of the North Sea took her break away. She had never imagined anything so wonderful. It lay before her like a great, grey shining animal, heaving quietly as it slept. But closer to the shore, she could see rough grey waves breaking on black rocks, great swathes of seaweed being tossed in the air by the incoming tide, then gleaming stretches of sand.

She sat staring as they travelled on and hugged herself in delight. Whatever experiences the next few weeks brought her, good or bad, no one could ever take this memory away from her.

Her thoughts turned at last to her young charge, Matilda. She had imagined she would be called Lady Matilda but Lydia Allerton had soon dispelled those ideas on their long drive up to Newcastle.

"No, of course not, Catherine, have you had no education? Sir Robert is just a baronet, not a baron. His children take no title. His wife would have been Lady Courtney if she had lived until he inherited and so will be his new one when he marries."

"And is he a pleasant type of man, cousin? I'm afraid I did not have the chance to make his acquaintance at the wedding."

Lydia had shrugged; she felt peevish. Sir Robert had not asked her to dance at the party. Indeed, he seemed to have gone out of his way to avoid her. She had little time for men who paid her no attention even though her own daughter was now related to him.

"A dull sort, in my opinion. No doubt thinks himself very grand, being a Sir. His brothers have all the charm in that family, although I still believe that my Cassandra would have done better marrying one of the officers in the regiment rather than that young doctor of hers. She will not have a very exciting life, that is for sure."

"Do you know anything of his daughter? The little girl who is to be in my charge?"

Lydia had been busy sorting through her reticule and was not paying great attention. "Her name is Matilda, I believe...I've heard she is a sulky child...I do so loathe sulky children...someone told me she rarely speaks, if ever. She needs a good beating. That would soon make her speak again."

Now, sitting next to the chickens, aching in every muscle from the jolting of the trap, Catherine wondered once more about Matilda. She was obviously going to be a very different type of child from Harriet whose constant chatter often gave her a headache.

She couldn't understand why Cousin Elizabeth and Mama Collins thought she would be the right person to care for her. Although she had to admit she had once overheard Mama Collins speaking to her father, saying that although she was not blessed with good looks, Catherine had an abundance of commonsense. So hopefully that would be enough. It was a great responsibility.

The long journey and the steady jolting finally took their toll and, slumped against the sack of potatoes, she fell into an uneasy sleep. She woke with a start when Donald shouted over his shoulder. "We're nearly there, Miss. Just coming through the village."

Catherine blinked herself awake; her bonnet had slipped down from her head and was held by its ribbons at the back of her neck. Luckily, she had so many pins in her hair that was braided tightly in two big coils that only a few wisps had so far escaped.

She gazed round, curious and interested. They were making their way along a rough track that wound through a small fishing village. Little cottages lined one side, huddled together, their windows shuttered against the east wind, gazed blindly out to sea. On the other side of the track there were brightly painted boats pulled up on the stones away from the water; she was vaguely aware of men mending nets and the crash of waves on the shoreline.

But it was the building in front of her that took Catherine's attention. They were climbing out from the village now, the track winding through slopes of rough grass, strewn with great grey boulders and tiny wild flowers. The pony was trotting quickly, obviously anxious for his own stable.

The road led over a wooden bridge across a moat filled with dark silent water, towards an open entrance door of nail studded wood. The walls of the castle were of rough grey stone and round towers stood at each end of the square building that stood on high ground, facing out towards the tumbling waves that crashed on rocks beneath steep cliffs . She could hear the calling of wild sea birds and the cawing of more familiar crows as they trotted through the gateway and into a courtyard beyond.

Catherine was aware of stables and barns on one side and the rest of the castle rose up in a square of three stories with battlements along the roof line. A flagpole stood above the gate, a black and red flag flapping vigorously in the sea breeze. Yes, it certainly didn't have the sprawling majesty of Alnwick, but it was still a castle and she was going to live there!

She could feel excitement bubbling up inside her, she was eager to meet Sir Robert and Matilda, eager to make a good first impression and show that she was a sensible, responsible person, a good companion for his little girl.

Sir Robert Courtney was sitting in the office next door to the stables, watching as his daughter played with wooden animals on the table next to him. Wanting her to be ready to welcome her new governess, he had searched for Matilda in her nursery but found it empty. All his fears for her safety had risen up inside him and he had spoken sharply to her nursery maid who had apparently left the child alone for a few minutes.

His relief when he had found her outside of the castle walls, stroking the great dray horses in the stables, had made him sound angry when he spoke to her. He knew he was being overly protective but she was all he had left in the world. If he lost Matilda, he didn't know what he would do. He made a point of seeing the child every day, to try and get her to talk to him or make some comment. But she rarely smiled and didn't speak.

"Matilda! You are not listening to me, I think. You must not run off like this and hide in the stables. You are a young lady and must act as such." There was silence. Sighing he went on, "Would you care to wait outside to greet your new governess? She is due any minute, if she has had a good journey from Alnwick. It is a Miss Collins who is arriving today, from Derbyshire. That is a very long way away. There is a map of England on my desk in my study - shall we go in and find Derbyshire on it?"

But there was no response.

Suddenly, from outside in the courtyard, there came the sound of hooves. Sir Robert stood up, sighing with relief. That would be the pony trap bringing the Miss Collins, whom Elizabeth Darcy had written was a distant relation of hers, a staid, responsible, caring girl; perhaps she could do something to make Matilda talk again. At least give the child some discipline and her lessons; he was scared she was becoming illiterate as well as dumb.

"What the good Lord – " There was a cacophony of noise from the yard. A woman was shouting "Catch them! Catch them! Don't let pony step on them!" Chickens squawked, a pony neighed and chaos seemed to be abroad in the calm world of Courtney castle.

He flung open the door and stared in amazement. A girl he recognized as one of the maids from Pemberley, the one he had seen dancing around the fountain in an abandoned manner, was now running round his stable yard, minus her bonnet, trying to catch a whole brood of yellow chicks that were hopping and fluttering in all directions. Two chickens were flying about, feathers filling the air, their crates smashed on the ground. A couple of kitchen maids were trying to shoo them into a corner whilst grooms and other servants stood around, laughing.

"Silence! Stop this charade at once! Everyone get back to work. And you, Miss, Miss...will you please put down that chick and tell me what you are doing here!"

He gazed round the yard, expecting to see the sensible female relative whom Elizabeth Darcy had promised to send north to help him. She must have dispatched this serving girl as chaperone on the journey. But the yard was now emptying as order was restored and the only female left was the slight figure with braided hair that was now adorned with two small chicken feathers, a smudge of what looked like potato earth on her cheek, holding a little yellow bird in her cupped hands.

"Sir, I do apologize most profusely," Catherine said now, coming across the cobbles to him, watching where she put her feet as she picked her way through more chicks. "It is all my fault. I was so eager to arrive that I didn't realise my foot had fallen asleep from being cramped up next to the chicken crates and so I overturned them as I jumped from the cart and - " She looked up as she spoke and stopped abruptly. "Oh! It's you!"

Catherine couldn't believe her eyes. The Sir Robert Courtney whom she was to work for was the same man who had been so curt and dismissive on the day of Cassandra's wedding. This was Richard's elder brother, the man she wanted so much to impress who was now looking at her with amazement and dislike.

"What is your name, girl?"

Catherine stiffened at his tone and pulled herself up to her full height. She did not want to appear disrespectful in any way, but she was the daughter of a gentleman and the granddaughter of Sir William Lucas. It was important that she made that clear.

"My name, Sir, is Miss Catherine Collins. My father is Mr William Collins, a gentleman and cleric who owns the living of Meryton in Hertfordshire; I am a distant cousin to Mrs Elizabeth Darcy of Pemberley who is my godmother and Mrs Cassandra Courtney your sister-in-law."

Sir Robert started to speak, then stopped. He ran his fingers through his dark hair and Catherine wondered if she ought to tell him that he now had a piece of straw entwined over his ear. A slight touch on Catherine's arm made her look round. A small girl with long blonde hair and big blue eyes was standing at her elbow, her beautiful face solemn.

"Matilda, go indoors at once and change into a clean dress. Ask Bessie to bring you down to the drawing-room when you are ready to be seen."

Catherine wanted to introduce herself, but realised much had to be sorted out before that could occur. Instead she gently handed the little fluffy chick into the girl's hands and said quietly, "Perhaps you would be kind enough to return this to its mother before you go, Matilda," and was rewarded by a quick upward flash from the dark blue eyes the child had inherited from her father.

"Come inside, Miss Collins. It is starting to rain and we cannot conduct our conversation out here in the stable yard."

Catherine followed him across the cobbles, almost running to keep up with his long-legged stride. He led her to the side of the castle directly opposite the main gate. Steps led up to an entrance that was guarded by two large, snarling stone lions and passing through the doorway she found herself in a great raftered hall. Passages stretched away into the gloom and above her head she could see galleried corridors on three sides. Suits of armour stood in the corners and several large portraits of gentlemen in uniform graced the stone walls with patterns of spears and axes displayed between. It was a dark, sombre place; no attempt had been made to lighten or decorate it to lift the spirit.

Sir Robert was standing impatiently at a doorway and she followed him into what she supposed was his study - dark wood and leather, hunting prints adorned the walls and two old dogs looked up lazily from where they lay in front of a smouldering fire and woofed gently at her. One got up and came over to sniff and lick her hand before settling down again.

'And that,' Catherine thought dryly, 'is the warmest welcome to my new home I have yet received!'

Sir Robert threw himself into a chair behind his desk and stared at the small, brown-haired woman in front of him. He could see that she was in her early twenties, not as young as he had first thought but she still did not look old enough to be a governess. And Elizabeth Darcy had promised someone responsible.

She was well dressed; her cloak was obviously expensive, although the heavy dark blue jacket and skirt she was wearing had seen better days, but all he could see when he looked at this Catherine Collins was her dancing in the garden at Pemberley, her hair loose and flying in the wind, the brown gleaming with bronze and chestnut hues as the early sunlight caught her in its beam.

"Miss Collins, I am sorry if I mistook you for a servant when we met at Pemberley but your apparel misled me and I spoke out of turn. You seem very young for this position, although your cousin assures me you will suit the role admirably."

Catherine had regained her composure and was trying to seem as dignified as she could, although that was difficult because there was a loose chicken feather tickling her ear.

"It is very good of her to say so. I will do my best to be of help and undertake the duties you require of me."

Sir Robert picked up a pile of papers, straightened them and put them down again. "I assure you, I do understand the family connection and that you are related to my new sister-in-law, Cassandra."

"Very distantly, Sir, yes. But whatever my connections, I am here to help care for your daughter, whom I suppose I met just now outside."

Getting up abruptly, Sir Robert walked to the window and stared out, turning his back on his visitor. This room looked out onto the courtyard where a groom was brushing rain water away from the cobbles. The clouds had passed over and the sky was a pale washed blue.

He took a deep breath, knowing he had to speak of things that were painful to him.

"Let me explain the situation, Miss Collins. As you may know, I inherited the castle and title just a few months ago when my father died and I moved back here with Matilda from our previous home. My brothers and sister and I were all born and raised in the castle and I lived here until my marriage. My wife and I then moved to Courtney Hall which is a small manor house a few miles away north along the coast. Matilda was born there. I lost my wife two years ago in an accident, one in which my daughter was involved. She was unharmed physically, thank God, but since then she has not spoken. Not a word."

Catherine impulsively stretched out a hand to his unyielding back, and then pulled it away, not realising that he had seen her action reflected in the window. "That is dreadful, Sir."

"Yes, but she must still learn to be a lady, to know her sums and write and read. I wish for her to be proficient in art, music and needlework. We attend church every Sunday in the local village and she kneels to pray every evening when she goes to bed, although she does not speak out loud, of course. I believe her to be intelligent and she is my only child."

He turned round to face her, wiping all emotion from his expression. "I may well marry again soon but until that is all settled, I wish for her to have a female companion and governess."

"Do you and Matilda live alone in the castle, Sir?"

"No, there is my Aunt Honoria. She is very elderly but still a formidable presence. She came to Richard's wedding - you might have noticed her sitting in the front pew at the church, wearing an extremely large purple hat - but perhaps you were not introduced. I believe she retired to her room following the service." A grim smile crossed his face. "She helped bring up myself, my brothers and my sister when our mother died, but she is far too old to have any control over Matilda, who seems to do exactly what she wants."

"Most children of that age like to be free, running around and playing."

Sir Robert frowned. "Now that is an example of what I mean when I say I need someone responsible to look after her. I will not have her in any danger. For example, I found her in the stables just now, giving carrots to my work horses! They are great creatures with immense strength that could have trodden her underfoot. And only last week, while I was at Pemberley, I'm told she left the castle and was traced to the fishing village. She was playing on the rocks! It makes my blood run cold to imagine it."

Catherine stood in silence. She was very tired and this irritating man had not even asked about her journey or offered her a seat. She was very tempted to tell him that she would ask for the pony and trap to take her back to Alnwick in the morning and go home to Longbourn, whether Mama Collins wanted her nor not. But at the same time she felt a wave of sympathy for Sir Robert. He obviously cared deeply for his daughter, even if he was being over protective. Hopefully, when he married, his new wife would sort out everything to everyone's advantage.

"Sir, from our earlier meeting, you may think I am irresponsible, but I can assure you I am not. I would do my best for Matilda and keep her safe. If I might suggest that I stay for a week and if you are still unhappy about my character, then I will return home. And - " she felt herself swaying with weariness but forced herself to stand still - "if I might be shown to my room, I would be very grateful. It has been an extremely long journey and I am very tired, smell of chickens and would like to wash!"

Sir Robert felt a flush cross his cheeks. This slip of a female was almost accusing him of being discourteous. What was wrong with him? He hadn't even offered her a seat and he could see now that she was trying hard to keep upright. Why hadn't the silly girl mentioned she was tired before? Most of his lady friends and acquaintances would have sunk down into a chair uninvited.

"Certainly, Miss Collins. That seems like a sensible compromise. I apologize for keeping you standing here." He turned and pulled the bell rope behind his desk. "My housekeeper, Mrs Crawford, will show you to your room. I have arranged that you take your meals with Matilda except for dinner of course, which is usually served to the family after she has gone to bed. The times will be explained to you and her routine which I insist you do not alter."

"Of course. Thank you, Sir."

"I do hope you do not find her company too distressing. I know some people are annoyed that she does not talk when, before the accident, she chattered away like a squirrel to all and sundry."

The door opened and a small, chubby cheeked woman dressed in black with a lace collar came in. Catherine smiled at her, curtseyed to Sir Robert and turned to go. She had just reached the door when she stopped and said, "Does Matilda make any sounds at all, Sir?"

The reply was brief and curt. "Sometimes, if say she falls over, she cries. But no words. She refuses to speak. The doctors say she can but she won't and I can't force her to do so. My youngest brother, Richard, whom of course you will have met at the wedding, is as you know, a doctor and he has even taken advice from the great specialists in London and Edinburgh, but no one can help."

Catherine started to speak, then shook her head and followed the housekeeper out into the main hall. She didn't fully understand because she was sure that as Matilda had run off with the chick clutched in her hands, she had heard her giggle.

3

Mrs Crawford had worked at Courtney Castle for more years than she cared to remember.

She had arrived there from her home in Morpeth as a young scullery maid and worked her way up to be housekeeper for Sir Edgar. She had seen the castle through good times and bad, watched as the four Courtney children had run wild after their mother's demise and been pleased and thankful when Lady Honoria arrived to take charge.

But although the children's behaviour had been somewhat tamed under her strict regime, Sir Edgar had fallen more and more into despair and lethargy, shunning company, retreating to his study and his books, not apparently caring if the building collapsed around his ears or the estate went to wrack and ruin. Saddened by his death, she had been relieved to see Sir Robert arrive with his young daughter.

The tragedy of Lucinda Courtney's death the year before had struck everyone on the estate very hard. Many had known her when she was one of the children who played on the beach with the Courtneys or run with their dogs across the moors.

If Mrs Crawford were completely honest, she hadn't cared greatly for her; there was something wild and disturbing under the beautiful front she showed to the world. Mrs Crawford had not been at all surprised by the accident; she had seen for herself when Lucinda had driven over to the castle from the Hall, how she loved to push the horses to their limits, glorying in the speed and danger.

Well, it had been God's will to take her and leave the poor little child without a voice. Life had to go on and the unspoken word was that an heir to the Courtney estate was required sooner rather than later. Mrs Crawford was fond of Mr Martin but dreaded him inheriting if anything dire were to happen to his brother. He had no real affection for the castle; his life was spent in London and it was rumoured that it was a life of gambling and dissolution.

She was not alone amongst the servants in welcoming the idea of a new Lady Courtney, one with a fortune at her disposal. It had seemed a foregone conclusion that Miss Richmond would be the person so honoured. Rich, elegant, witty, already a close friend to Sir Robert and the other family members, it had been quite obvious that, at a seemly time, Miss Richmond would be the chosen one. But until then, could this young lady help make Matilda's life easier? Although she was small and looked inoffensive, she already seemed to have annoyed Sir Robert which was not a good start.

"As Sir Robert would have told you, my name is Mrs Martha Crawford," the housekeeper said cheerfully as she led Catherine up a narrow flight of spiral stone stairs that were built inside one of the castle turrets. "I hope you'll be happy here, Miss Collins."

"I hope so, too, Mrs Crawford." She wondered how long it would take her to run up and down this stairway without getting out of breath. The housekeeper was almost a whole turn ahead of her and there was no time to gaze out of the slit arrow windows to look at the view.

"It's a fine old place and the master is a good man. Old Sir Edgar was a hard taskmaster, but that's not to say we weren't sad when he went just after New Year. He had been ailing for some considerable time."

"One of my distant cousins is lately married to Dr Richard Courtney," Catherine said, feeling it important that she made her place in the castle clear from the start.

"Ah, yes Miss, that is what I was told by Sir Robert. Miss Cassandra or Mrs Courtney as I must call her now. I do hear she is a pretty young girl."

Catherine stopped for a second to get her breath as they left the spiral steps through a small door onto a long straight corridor. She realised they were now high up on one side of the great hall. "Indeed she is. I was at the wedding; that was where I met Sir Robert."

She thought it best not to describe the circumstances. She had no idea how much the staff of Courtney Castle gossiped about their employers, but she imagined it was the same as any other household!

"Ah, I'm right pleased Master Richard has found himself a nice wife. There was a lot of unhappiness when he left here to become a doctor, but he was always a studious boy. Sir Robert was always wanting to be out and about on the estate and as for Mr Martin - well! Least said the better about that young man!

"Now, Miss Collins, as you will see, the castle is built around two great halls, divided by the ballroom which has been shut up this many a year. We are above the south hall, where you came in. Upstairs, here, is what is called the South Wing, it leads between the staircase where we came up and the East Wing where the family have their rooms."

Catherine saw that the corridor had a wooden panel on one side and closed doors on the other. She peered over the waist high balustrade and looked down into the hall. It seemed a great distance away. Shivering, she turned back to the housekeeper.

"The staff and Miss Matilda use the spiral staircase, as will you, of course. Be careful going down, the stone steps can be slippery. The other turret has various rooms on each floor. On the far side of the castle is an open stairway that descends into the north hall. The family and any guests use that one as it is closer for them.

She took a breath and walked briskly along the passageway with Catherine scurrying to keep up. "Now, just along here is your new home, with the nursery next door and the night nursery after that. There are connecting doors between all three rooms, so you do not need to keep walking in and out into the corridor.

"Miss Matilda has a nursery maid, Bessie Stokes. She gets our young lady up every morning and makes sure she is washed and dressed in time for breakfast. She has been putting her to bed every evening, too, and sleeps in a little alcove just off her room. Bessie deals with her washing. She'll take care of yours too, of course. I hope you find her satisfactory - she came with Sir Robert and Miss Matilda when they moved into the castle when Sir Edgar died. She comes from a fishing village just north of here and I think her training is sadly lacking. She doesn't always know her place in my opinion."

"I'm sure she and I will get along splendidly," Catherine said hopefully.

Mrs Crawford hesitated. "You will not be needing a maid of your own, will you, Miss? There is no one in the household trained for that, I'm afraid and Sir Robert never..."

"No, certainly not," Catherine broke in swiftly, feeling her cheeks flush. "I am quite capable of caring for myself." And she tried to stop herself from smiling as she imagined confronting her employer and asking for a personal maid to help her dress and put up her hair!

Her room was large and square, pleasantly decorated in a rather old-fashioned style with a large bed tucked into one corner. The windows in the grey stone wall were small and arched with tiny panes of glass, but there was a fire burning in the grate to ward off the chill April air and her trunk had already been brought up and was ready for her to unpack.

Mrs Crawford ran her finger along the mantlepiece to check for dust and seemed to be happy with what she didn't find. "I'll leave you to get settled. Dinner will be at seven but I expect you'll wanting to meet Miss Matilda first. I believe Bessie had instructions to change her dress and take her to the drawing-room. If you go back down the stairs, you'll find it to your right, next door to the breakfast-room."

She smiled at the slight figure standing in front of her. She had been expecting someone very different - Sir Robert had informed her that he was sending for a governess and in Mrs Crawford's experience, that usually meant a lady in her thirties or forties who would be only too keen to make sure the servants knew she was not one of them, that although she was not 'family' she was definitely not staff.

She had been prepared for battle but somehow, although this small, brown haired girl with big brown eyes that were wide with apprehension had commented on her relationship to the new Mrs Courtney, she offered no feeling of superiority. It was odd that she had somehow managed to annoy Sir Robert and the housekeeper made her way downstairs, wondering if there was more to Miss Catherine Collins than met the eye.

When Mrs Crawford left, Catherine went straight to the window and gazed out. She realised that the castle must stand on a small promontory, jutting out from the land into the ocean. Looking down and along the coastline, she could see the rooftops of the distant fishing village they had driven through. Dark grey waves were breaking on rocks beneath her. Showers of spray rose and fell relentlessly and she shivered as the window rattled violently in its frame as the east wind buffeted the building.

The water in the washbasin was tepid, but enough to wash her hands and face. She re-braided her hair, pulling it back severely from her face, hoping the style made her look older and reliable. She was horrified to find small chicken feathers as she worked and hoped desperately that they hadn't been apparent to Sir Robert.

She changed swiftly from her travelling clothes into one of the dresses she had been given by Bennetta Darcy. It was far more fashionable than anything she usually wore, with a pulled in waist, several petticoats to fill the material of the skirt and fuller sleeves which tightened round her wrists. Probably not the usual apparel for a governess but the dark pink material was warm and Catherine was beginning to realise that having lived in the south all her life, she would have to get used to the different temperatures in the north of England. She draped a paler pink shawl around her shoulders and stared at her reflection in the looking-glass.

Sighing, she accepted that she could never be called pretty, but her face was not important at the moment. She wanted to appear mature and sensible but had a sinking feeling that she looked more like a young girl playing dress-up in her sister's clothes. She wondered why she felt uncomfortable wearing colours? Was it because browns and greys summed up the sort of person she was? Girls who wore bright clothes were usually vivacious and outgoing, like Bennetta - not quiet and sensible.

Just then there was a knock on the door from her room to the schoolroom and a tall girl in a nursery maid's pale green uniform came in, dropping a small curtsey. Catherine could see that she had dark ginger hair, tied up under her cap and very green eyes.

"Hello, you must be Bessie."

"That's right. And you be Miss Collins, the governess." The girl had a very strong accent, the same as Donald, the boy who'd driven the pony trap.

"I'm pleased to meet you. I shall rely on you to tell me about Miss Matilda's likes and dislikes," Catherine said. "I hope we can work together to care for her."

"I've looked after her since the day she were born."

Catherine hesitated. She could hear the resentment in the other girl's voice and realised that she would have to tread very carefully. Bessie Stokes obviously had every right to feel aggrieved, to resent being replaced in some aspects of Matilda's care. But it was obvious from the girl's speech that she was not educated and could not possibly teach Matilda all she needed to know.

"And I'm sure she is very fond of you. How unhappy the dreadful accident to her mother must have made her."

Bessie tucked her hands inside her white apron. "It might not be my place to say, but Madam had no right to take Miss Matilda out in that phaeton. Dangerous things they are. Tip over at the slightest corner and Madam always drove too fast."

Catherine hesitated to gossip but this was interesting. "Mrs Courtney was driving herself?"

"Aye, Miss, that she was. Just her and my little lady. Took a corner too fast, the traces broke, the horse bolted off and they crashed down a slope. She died there but my little lady was thrown clear and was found, just sitting on the grass, not a scratch on her. A miracle, it was."

"A miracle indeed. Well, Bessie, I will do all I can to help you and I'm sure you will do the same for me. We both have Miss Matilda's well-being as our priority."

Bessie nodded, then, as a sign maybe of a truce, said, "I'll finish your unpacking for you, then, Miss Collins."

Catherine nodded her thanks. She would have preferred to do so herself, but knew when an olive branch was being offered. She had the feeling that she was going to need all the friendly gestures she could find in this great, cold place.

Realising that some time had now passed, she ran down the turret stairway, the steepness taking her faster and faster as she flew round the corners and erupted at speed into the hall, thankful that there was no one around to see her but enjoying the excitement of the descent.

Catching her breath, she smoothed her skirts and unaware that her cheeks were now glowing as pink as her dress, walked sedately into the drawing-room. Once again Catherine was aware of grey stone walls and black raftered ceiling, but at least the floor was highly polished wood and the furniture, although heavy in design, looked comfortable. A great fireplace held logs that threw out a welcome heat and she was delighted to see an elegant piano-forte in a corner, its charming, elegant design looking out of place amongst the masculine furnishings.

Sir Robert was sitting on a sofa, a lock of dark hair falling across his forehead, watching as Matilda played on the floor with two raggedy dolls. The old dogs were lying in front of the fire, asleep. He didn't seem to hear Catherine and she had time to study the expression of sadness in his dark eyes before he realised she was in the room.

"Miss Collins - come across to the fire. It is cold for April. Matilda - stand up, child. Shake hands with Miss Collins, your new governess. Make a nice curtsey. I know you can."

The little girl did exactly what she was told, although she kept her head down, her blonde hair falling over her pale cheeks so Catherine could not see her expression.

"Hello, Matilda. I am so pleased to meet you again. I do hope we will be great friends. I hope the little chick got back to its mother safely?"

There was no reply, just the upward flash of bright blue eyes under the cascade of curls. The hand in hers was cold and thin and quickly taken away and the little girl sat on the floor again, cradling her dolls, the fire flickering bright lights onto her hair.

Sir Robert gestured to a chair and Catherine sat, folding her hands in her lap. "I'm afraid you will get nothing out of her, Miss Collins. Hopefully things will improve. I intend to be here for a few days to make sure you have settled in and established a good routine with Matilda and then I shall be away from Courtney for a short while. I want her to have a good grounding in reading and to know her letters and numbers. She will be seven this summer. She likes to paint and draw, and I am keen to discover if she has inherited my late wife's musical ability. If so, I intend to hire a teacher for her."

"I will do my very best. "

"Well, that can all be arranged when I return."

"And do you go far, Sir?"

"No, only a few miles or so." He sounded irritated and Catherine wondered if she had been wrong to ask, but it had seemed a fairly innocuous question. He had fallen silent and she gazed round the room, desperately trying to find something to talk about. Above the mantlepiece was an oil painting of a beautiful young woman. She stared at it, admiring the perfect porcelain skin, curls of yellow hair. Every line of the woman showed grace and elegance.

Sir Robert caught her glance. "My late wife, Lucinda," he said briefly and Catherine could hear the pain in his voice.

"She was very lovely, Sir."

"Indeed. I think Matilda has a look of her but even I can see that she will never have that wonderful beauty. I wish her to grow up to be just like her mother. That is her piano-forte over there. Lucinda played so well; it was a delight to hear her. I do hope Matilda has inherited some of her talent - I am afraid I have none myself."

Catherine nodded, then said practically. "Well, I imagine she will have her own abilities, things she likes to do or not, as we all do." She felt a wave of sympathy for Matilda if this standard of perfection was what she was always to be held to throughout her life.

"We cannot always do what we wish to do," came the terse reply and he stood up and walked across the room to a writing table and picked up some papers. "We all have duties to our parents and our families, whether we like them or not."

Catherine bit her lip, holding back the words that would probably have seen her on the next carriage out of Courtney Castle. She really did not know what was wrong with her. She never usually had any inclination to argue with people. She wondered if the long journey had upset her disposition in some way and could only hope that the next day would see her return to her usual staid self.

"Encourage her to speak as much as you can. The doctors, including my brother, tell me there is no physical reason for her not to talk." He sighed. "You would be surprised at all the differing advice I have been given about Matilda. But I am her father and I want to keep her safe and well. She is not to run wild around the castle. It is a dangerous place for a child."

This time Catherine couldn't help herself. "But you and your brothers and sister grew up here, didn't you, Sir? Without any disasters?"

Sir Robert thought briefly of swimming in the sea, climbing rocks, catching tiny green crabs in pools and then put all those memories firmly aside.

"That is no reason for me to allow Matilda to do the same. My brothers and I were lucky - we had my elder sister, Susannah, who kept a close eye on us and stopped our more adventurous escapades before we could come to any real harm. But Matilda is a little girl with no siblings or playmates and I have no intention of allowing her to run wild and put herself in danger. I trust I make myself clear, Miss Collins?"

"Perfectly, Sir."

He gazed suspiciously at her down turned eyes and demure demeanour. It wasn't that he thought she was lying to him, just that somewhere inside him he doubted if this girl was the calm disciplinarian that Elizabeth Darcy had promised him.

Just then the door swung open and a very elderly lady, dressed all in dark purple, including her cap, walked slowly and laboriously into the room, leaning on an ebony walking-stick. Sir Robert leapt to her side and Catherine automatically stood up.

"Aunt Honoria, this is a pleasure. We seldom see you downstairs in the afternoon. Matilda, come and make your curtsey."

"Bah! Leave the child where she is. I don't want her underfoot. I'll like most trip over her and then there will be ructions. Help me to a chair, Robert. I came down to inspect this young lady, as no one had the courtesy to bring her up to see me."

"I apologize. I thought you might be resting."

"I can rest in my grave, can't I? Come here, gal. What's your name? I was told but it's slipped my memory. Sent by Elizabeth Darcy, eh? Well, she's got more sense than most women these days. Let me look at you. Going to take care of Matilda, eh? Make her talk? Is that what you think?"

"Countess Honoria de Bois - Miss Catherine Collins. Aunt Honoria is my father's sister. She kindly came to look after us when my mother died and has been at Courtney ever since."

Catherine curtsied, aware of two very black, beady eyes looking her up and down. Undaunted, she straightened up and returned the gaze, surprised to find that the eyes were now twinkling, as if the old lady wanted to laugh.

"Yes, I had four to look after and little limbs of Satan they were, too. Except Susannah, she was the only one to be trusted, poor plain creature. And now look at her, no husband, having to live with one of her brothers, never to have a home of her own. Well, well, I expect that will be Matilda's fate, too, if she doesn't find her voice quickly. I've suggested you put her on a diet of bread and water for a week or so. She'd learn to talk if she were hungry. Pandering to the child will do no good at all."

"I will do my best to care for Matilda in every way," Catherine said firmly. "I have a little sister and am quite at ease with small children. I am sure Matilda will speak when she has something important to say."

"Hmmmph, do you now? Important, eh? What could a child have to say that is of any importance? We'll see, we'll see. Robert, have you rung for tea and cake? Do I have to beg for sustenance now?"

Catherine felt the merest flicker of a smile hover around her lips. Sir Robert looked flustered, far more approachable than his usual severe demeanour. Then she realised he was looking directly at her and with the smallest flick of his head, pointed to Matilda. It was obvious that he wanted his daughter taken out of the room.

"If you will excuse me, Lady Honoria, Sir Robert, I will take this opportunity of allowing Matilda to show me her rooms and all her possessions." She held out her hand and the little girl stood up immediately and ran across the room to her side and with a brief curtsey Catherine escorted her out.

As she was closing the door behind her, she paused as Matilda dropped one of her dolls and stooped to retrieve it. She couldn't hear Sir Robert's words, just the rumble of his voice, but Honoria de Bois' was quite clear.

"I thought you were looking for someone staid and reliable. Bah! You've no more sense where women are concerned now then you did when you married that flighty Lucinda!"

Catherine escorted Matilda upstairs, pondering over the people who lived in this cold, dreary place. Sir Robert loved his daughter, that was obvious, but it was a love born out of loss. She was sure he had no idea at all what the child was really like. He just wanted a copy of his lost Lucinda.

What of the old lady? A relic of a different time with no patience for a child with a problem. So where was the fun and laughter that a youngster needed in their lives? As far as Catherine could see, it was going to be down to her to provide it and she was beginning to realise it would not be an easy task.

4

Catherine did not sleep well that night. The bed was comfortable, she had no complaints about her room, but the long journey, the shock of finding that the man who had chided her in the Pemberley gardens was the man she must now work with and her concern about Matilda - all of these kept her tossing and turning.

She rose as soon as dawn broke, the sun rising and bathing her windows early with light. Determined to make a good impression as a sensible governess, she found a plain brown muslin, trimmed with dark blue, high collared and long sleeved. Braiding her hair as tightly as she could, she pinned it to her head as hard as was possible - this was not the morning for loose tresses. She gazed at herself in the mirror: today she would be the very best governess she could be and would refrain from argument or discussion with Sir Robert because she obviously had the ability to annoy him.

A knock at her door heralded Bessie with Matilda.

"She didn't sleep well," the girl said abruptly. "Tossed and turned all night, poor lamb."

"I expect she is as apprehensive as I am about today," Catherine said and smiling, held out her hand to the child. "It is always difficult to make new friends, isn't it, Matilda? But you must remember that you know all about the castle and I am just a stranger who will need your help." She inspected the little girl and raised her eyebrows to Bessie. Matilda was wearing a very frilly pink dress, far too fancy for a morning's attire.

"She would wear it, Miss," Bessie said with a sigh. "Pulled off her nice plain blue dress and threw it on the floor. I reckon Sir Robert will say it's my fault, not being able to control her."

Catherine was about to chide her pupil when she suddenly caught sight of herself in the mirror and smiled instead. "I think we have both decided to look our very best this morning, Bessie. I agree it is not suitable for breakfast, but surely Sir Robert will not be too concerned. And if he is, I will explain. No one will blame you, believe me."

She held out her hand and, after a moment's pause, Matilda grasped it. "It is a very pretty dress, Matilda. You may wear it for breakfast but perhaps change afterwards in case it gets dirty."

Bessie's green eyes gleamed. This Miss Collins might be small and slight but she had a very determined expression and Bessie had the hope that she might be good for Matilda. Hurriedly she spoke again.

"I meant to warn you, Miss." She nodded down towards the little girl. "We have problems with eating of our breakfast at the moment. Last couple of weeks she's done no more than drink her milk. Won't touch a bite of anything else. Sir Robert gets right scratchy about it. I leave her to eat with him and he rings for me to collect her and I can tell there's been argument. But perhaps as you'll be eating with her, she'll behave."

Catherine sighed. She knew only too well from living with her Harriet that small children could be extremely annoying when they decided they disliked a certain food.

When they reached the breakfast-room, they found Sir Robert still at the table, drinking coffee, a book propped up in front of him.

"Good morning, Miss Collins. I hope you slept well? Good morning, sweetheart!" He held out his arms to Matilda who ran up for a kiss. Catherine could see him frowning as he looked at the pink dress and hoped and prayed he wouldn't comment.

"We are determined to show the world that we are happy today," she said as she took her seat next to Matilda.

Sir Robert frowned, then smiled and gestured for a footman to pour Catherine a cup of hot chocolate. The table was laden with breads, cheeses and meats and a large covered dish in the centre. The footman removed the lid and ladled out a dish of thick grey porridge into a bowl and placed it in front of Matilda.

"My aunt is a great believer in porridge for growing children," Sir Robert said, aware of the look on his daughter's face. "She says it is good for their bones and brains and, who knows, it might help Matilda find her voice again. So she has decided that the child should have a bowl every morning."

Catherine cut herself a slice of cheese. "And do you also eat porridge, Sir? Perhaps if she sees you enjoying it, she will make an effort to do so as well."

"Me? No, can't stand the stuff. But if it helps Matilda, then she must do so, although I have to admit she doesn't seem to care for it. But she must learn discipline. I'm afraid we have been having the same problem every morning, but she is refused permission to leave the table until she has at least eaten three or four good spoonfuls."

The little girl was sitting motionless, her bottom lip pushed out, mutinously, and Catherine wondered with a sigh why it was considered unacceptable for children to have the same likes and dislikes as adults. But she could tell from the look of concern on Sir Robert's face that he thought he was doing his best for his daughter. Her health and well being were obviously of utmost importance to him and Catherine could sense the frustration he was experiencing.

He shut his book with a snap and stood up. "I can see we are going to have the same confrontation this morning. Matilda! Listen to Papa. You must eat some of your good porridge. It will do you good. Miss Collins, I leave you in charge. Please make sure that my instructions are adhered to in every aspect."

Catherine nodded but her heart sank. Forcing a child to eat was not the best way to gain it's trust and it was vital that Matilda liked and trusted her. She glanced over the table and her eyes gleamed as she caught sight of a jug full of honey and honeycomb.

"Look, Matilda, let's make a little castle with the porridge with a moat all around, just like here at Courtney. And this honey can fill in the moat!"

Swiftly she dug her own spoon into the thick grey porridge and began to sculpt it into a shape. It looked nothing like a castle, of course, but Matilda seemed to think it was and happily poured honey into the moat.

Catherine looked up to find the footman standing opposite her grinning as a spoonful of honey with a very little porridge attached was eaten. Then his face went blank and Catherine realised how narrow the path was between being a servant and being part of the family.

What she hadn't seen, but the footman had, was that the door had swung open silently and Sir Robert stood there, watching as his obstinate little girl cheerfully ate a large portion of her breakfast, even if it was heavily laden with pure honey from the Courtney hives.

He was about to enter, to comment on Miss Collin's success, but hesitated. That was the girl's job, of course, but he turned away, wondering why he hadn't thought of such a simple ploy himself. The picture of the two of them, their lips both gleaming, sticky with honey, stayed with him all day.

The morning was spent in the nursery with Catherine trying to discover exactly what Matilda already knew. To her surprise, the child had no trouble with simple sums written up on her slate and could copy all the words written out for her with ease. There was no way of knowing if she could read - she held the book and silently followed Catherine's finger as she spelt out the words - but she could certainly draw.

After a simple lunch served in the day nursery, they explored the grounds which stretched out inland from the great castle walls. Cows, pigs and chickens, paddocks for the horses, a large thriving vegetable patch - Catherine smiled to herself, knowing how much her papa would have liked to explore the growing cabbages and a small herb garden.

She talked to Matilda the whole time, explaining the names of the herbs, crumbling leaves between her fingers for the child to smell and was certain that the little girl understood her even though there was no reply.

The path from the herbs led down a flight of stone steps to a wooden door in a brick wall that opened with a creak under Catherine's touch. On the other side was a walled fruit and flower garden, sheltered from the harsh salt wind. It was sadly neglected: she thought it had been left untouched for several years and weeds were choking the beds. But the climbing roses and apple trees trained along the brick walls were already in bud and she could only imagine how lovely it must have looked years ago.

An elderly gardener, short and bent with a wrinkled brown face, appeared and although Catherine had great difficulty understanding his accent - not helped by the fact that he did not seem to have a tooth left in his mouth - she gathered his name was Jeremiah and he would be pleased to let the little mistress help in the garden. Catherine asked him for a few tools and with Matilda at her side, began to weed one of the flower beds, letting light in to the struggling plants.

"Look, Matilda, this can be your very own flower-bed," she said cheerfully. "Oh, here are some lovely red tulips, hidden by the bindweed. Let's rescue them. All the flowers we grow here you can pick for your bedroom. And perhaps I may take some for my room as well."

There was no reply, but it seemed to Catherine that Matilda attacked the weeds with even more enthusiasm. They were still busy when Sir Robert appeared unseen in the doorway, looking hot and irritable, his riding jacket over his arm, his shirt undone at the neck, his breeches dusty.

The headache and weariness that had plagued him all morning as he dealt with difficult farmer tenants vanished like summer mist as he stared into the wild garden, a place he had almost forgotten about. He knew his mother had had it built with red brick walls in this county of stone, to protect the flowers she loved so much from the north sea winds. And his sister, Susannah, had cared for it when she grew older. But since Susannah had left to live with their brother down in Derbyshire, it had been sadly neglected.

He stood quite still, a smile on the face that had found little humour in life for the past years. He could see two people, bent double, almost upside down, amongst the tulips. A white sun bonnet and a rather battered straw hat hid their faces, but he knew who was labouring so diligently and silently left them to their work, his heart a little lighter. Perhaps this Miss Collins had found something that would open up Matilda's heart and voice.

When Matilda tired of gardening, she tugged at Catherine's hand and led her into the stables. Donald, the young groom, was busy cleaning bridles and saddles and put down his rags and smiled warmly at Matilda.

"Ah, good afternoon Miss. I expect Miss Matilda be wanting to feed her favourites. They been a-waiting for her to come."

Catherine glanced around nervously, but there was no sign of Sir Robert and she felt it was unfair to stop the child from feeding the horses, as long as she was there to keep her safe. Matilda seemed fearless as the big heads swooped down over their stable doors to take carrots from her palm.

"She seems quite at ease in their company."

Donald grinned, his dark eyes gleaming in his tanned face. "She comes out here every day, Miss. I've been told it's forbidden, but she comes to no harm. I'd never let that happen. She's just a natural around the horses. Reckon her Ma was the same."

"You knew the late Mrs Courtney?"

"Aye, Miss." Donald frowned and watched closely as Matilda made her way along the long line of stalls, offering an apple or carrot to each occupant. "I was only a youngster of course. Had just started work in the stables at Courtney Hall. Mrs Courtney would bring the babee down to the stables to pat the horses when she was just a little mite. But after the accident, the Maister stopped her coming."

Matilda got to the end of the row and with a final pat to an elderly donkey who lived in the same stall as one of the Shires, finished her feeding and looked back in longing when, finally, Catherine urged her upstairs to the nursery.

After her supper, Bessie appeared to take her for a bath and put her to bed. Catherine would have enjoyed doing that, but she didn't want to upset the nursery maid. It was quite obvious that Matilda was very fond of the red-headed girl and she found her lying in bed while Bessie sat on a stool next to her, telling her a story in her odd local accent, about mermaids and great caverns made of emeralds and pearls until the child's eyes drooped and she fell asleep.

Catherine suddenly realised she was now having no difficulty in understanding the local dialect. She only feared that she might end up copying it herself!

"That was a lovely fairy tale, Bessie," Catherine said as the girl stood up and came through into the day nursery, her arms full of clothes to be washed.

"Learnt them all from my old Granma, Miss. She's a right one for all the old stories. Miss Matilda loves hearing them. Mrs Courtney used to bring her to see Granma when we lived at Courtney Hall. She'd sit for hours hearing tales of mermaids who granted you wishes if you saw one." She shot Catherine an indignant look. "It don't do any harm to tell her them again."

"No, no, of course it doesn't! You can tell she was happy to hear them. Now I know she likes mermaids, perhaps I'll try and draw one for her to copy, although as I have never seen one myself, that might prove difficult."

"As you will, Miss. I wouldn't want to get into any trouble over it. The new Lady Courtney might not like it."

"The new Lady Courtney?" Catherine didn't know why she was so surprised.

"Well, Maister must marry again, we all know that. He wants to give Miss Matilda a new mother and he needs a male heir or else the title will go to his brother if he should die. And like as not it will be Miss Abigail Richmond he marries. She's stayed here before and that's where he's going in a few days - to visit her. Rumour has it, she's been invited to stay for a while to get to know Miss Matilda better. Mrs Crawford is getting the best guest rooms ready."

"I see." Catherine couldn't understand why she felt so disconcerted at this news. It had always been made plain to her that Sir Robert wanted a companion for Matilda until the time he remarried. Maybe this was going to be sooner than she had imagined.

She was about to ask Bessie what Abigail Richmond was like then stopped herself. That was gossiping and she refused to indulge in such a pastime with a servant. She would meet the lady and make her own decision about her. She only hoped that Miss Richmond would love Matilda and care for her but surely Sir Robert would not marry anyone who could not do so.

As Catherine was dressing for dinner, a maid arrived with a message from Sir Robert, saying that he was dining out, his aunt was eating in her own rooms and so he had arranged for Catherine likewise to have her meal served upstairs.

Catherine was not sure whether she was pleased or not. She hadn't relished the idea of sitting opposite her employer and his terrifying aunt for a whole hour and had wondered what she could possibly talk about, but now, when the opportunity had gone she felt in some strange way bereft.

The second day followed the same pattern as the first, except that Sir Robert was not present at breakfast - she discovered that Matilda could do simple cross-stitch on her sampler which boded well for the future when she progressed to silks and embroidery stitches. There was no way to know if she was going to be musical, like her mother. In the drawing-room, Catherine played a few little tunes on the piano-forte but the child didn't show any desire to try it herself.

When Matilda had gone to bed, Catherine changed into another of Bennetta's dresses, this one a rather grand affair in green plaid and a thick lace collar and made her way down the spiral stairway again.

She had had little opportunity to explore the interior of the castle; she knew the kitchens - she had introduced herself to the cook, thanking her for her dinner, consulting her on plain meals that might appeal to Matilda - the sculleries and servants' dining-hall were in the basement. It was but a short walk from the doorway to the kitchen to the breakfast-room which she knew well. Beyond that was the drawing-room but dinner would obviously be served in the dining-room and so far she had had no reason to investigate.

After trying various locked doors, she discovered it on the side of the castle that faced the sea - a long, high-ceilinged, dark-raftered room whose windows were covered with heavy red drapes. Candles stood at intervals on chests and side tables but their light did little to make the room more home like. The paintings on the walls were dark and gloomy, mostly seeming to be either of shipwrecks and battles fought at sea between fleets of ships or still life portrayals of dead ducks and deer.

A long oak table was laid for dinner, with only one end being needed for the four place settings. A great stone fireplace did at least hold what looked like a whole tree trunk but the wood must have been wet because it hissed and crackled and gave out very little heat.

Catherine gazed around her, feeling subdued and sad. What a gloomy place for Matilda to call home. There wasn't a single attractive or genteel touch to be seen. Even Pemberley - that had larger and grander rooms and far more of them - felt more like a home than this sad castle.

A footman appeared, smiled briefly at her and held the door open for Countess Honoria. The elderly lady entered, dressed all in black with jet beading on her cap. Her fingers were heavy with rings, including one great ruby on her left hand. She was leaning heavily on her stick and barely acknowledged Catherine's curtsey as she passed, heading for a seat at the head of the table.

"Well, well, sit down, girl, sit down. The soup will be cold by the time my nephew gets here. We won't wait." She imperiously rang a small hand bell that was next to her plate and the door opened again for a footman carrying aloft a tray with a soup tureen.

Catherine waited as a portion was poured into her bowl and hesitated as Lady Honoria helped herself to bread and began to eat. It seemed so rude to begin without Sir Robert being present.

"Bah! It's already cold. I can't eat it." The old lady pushed her bowl aside and glared round the room.

"I suppose it does take quite a long time to get it here from the kitchen," Catherine ventured. There was a thin scum forming on the surface of her soup and she, too, pushed her bowl aside.

"That's why I usually eat in my room. Nice big fire in there even in the summer and I keep all the dishes hot on the hearth."

Catherine gazed round at the vast, grey stone room, the candles flickering in myriad draughts from ill-fitting windows. "This does seem a large place for a small family dinner, although I am sure it looks very grand when there are several people sitting down."

Lady Honoria grunted. "A long time since that's happened. When my sister-in-law was alive, Edgar gave big dinner parties and dances. Cheerful, jolly affairs, lots of food and drink. The ballroom was open and there was dancing, with musicians at the end of the room up on a little balcony. The children came in to say goodnight and be given candied fruit and sips of wine." She stared round the cold, empty room, remembering.

"It's a grand room but very bleak. I suppose most castle rooms are like that."

"Bah! Doesn't have to be. There used to be tapestries on the walls in here. Pictures of flowers, unicorns and deer and woods, from what I remember. Pretty bright colours. But Edgar had them taken down a few years before he died. Packed them away in one of the attics. He shut and locked the ballroom and vowed there would be no more music. I'm surprised he didn't shut this room too, but the children had to eat somewhere."

Catherine sighed. "But now Sir Robert could always use the breakfast room for dinner, I suppose."

Two beady black eyes pinned her to her seat. "Hmm, well, girl, Catherine isn't it, you can always ask him."

"Is Courtney Hall where Matilda was born a gloomy place?"

"No, I can't say it is." The old lady's tone was grudging. " I didn't care for Lucinda but she made the place a comfortable home. Had big windows put in, lots of light. Nursery all painted pale in a French fashion. Shut up now. I suppose in the very unlikely event of Martin taking a wife, it would become their home up here in Northumberland."

"Matilda must miss her mama."

"Well, if she does, she doesn't tell us, does she? Enough of this chit-chat. I'm going back to my room. I'll have the rest of my dinner sent up. When my nephew arrives tell him he's most remiss in being late. I am very displeased."

She started to get up and the footman rushed over to pull back her chair and offer help if she needed it, but she waved him away with an impatient gesture and without another word, left the room, leaning heavily on her stick.

Catherine sat silently as her soup bowl was removed and some chicken dish in a white sauce was placed before her. She was just murmuring her thanks when the door flew open and Sir Robert came in, looking hot and irritable and bringing with him the sharp scent of horse and leather. He was still wearing his riding clothes and had obviously not stopped to bathe. He pulled off his riding stock as he entered and threw it to one side, tugging open the top button of his shirt.

"My apologies, Miss Collins. I am damnably late for dinner, but my horse lost a shoe and I had to walk him the last two miles. I'm glad to see you have not waited for me." He flung himself down opposite her, so violently that the candles on the table flickered and danced.

"Did my aunt not come down to dine?"

"Yes, she did. But the soup was cold and she took exception to the dining-room and decided to eat upstairs."

"What's wrong with the room?" Sir Robert waved a footman over to fill his wine glass.

Catherine took a deep breath. "Oh nothing, Sir. It is a very imposing room. I love the ancient atmosphere given by the black beams and giant fireplace. Indeed, if you were giving a dinner for forty people, it would be wonderful. But if I may presume to say, it is a little gloomy and very cold. I know Matilda eats in the nursery at the moment but in a few years she will be old enough to have her meals with you down here and the atmosphere might prove a little overwhelming for a small girl. I was wondering if we could perhaps use the breakfast room instead while she is young. It is nearer the kitchens and so the food would stay warmer."

Sir Robert took a sip of wine and glanced sharply across the table to where the dancing candle light flickered on tightly braided hair and a green plaid dress that was a little too big and elaborate for the girl wearing it. "Oh, that's your opinion, is it, Miss Collins?"

Catherine forced herself to stay calm and glanced down at her plate where the chicken was now congealing in its sauce. Between them the members of the Courtney family seemed determined that she would not get anything to eat tonight except bread!

"Excuse me, I did not mean to be impertinent or to cast any disparagement on your home. I am just trying to see everything through Matilda's eyes. It makes no difference to me, of course, whether there are tapestries on the walls or flowers in the vases. I will obviously not be here long enough for it to matter."

"No indeed! I am well aware that you are only here for a short time. So perhaps you could kindly refrain from redecorating my home and concentrate on teaching my daughter."

Mortified, Catherine stood up so quickly that the footman had no time to move her chair and it rocked violently, almost crashing to the floor. "Of course, Sir, and I apologise if I have offended in any way. Now, if you will excuse me, I will leave you to your dinner. I am very fatigued and will retire early."

Sir Robert nodded and stood politely to watch her leave the table, trying hard not to notice or smile when he spotted her slipping some more bread in the pocket of her dress.

"I will be away from home for two weeks as from tomorrow. In the circumstances, I will arrange for all your meals to be taken in the breakfast room. I will ask Mrs Crawford to inform my aunt of the changes to our routine. Oh, and Miss Collins, pray take some cheese with you to eat with that bread. I would not want anyone living under my roof to go hungry!"

As the days passed, Catherine began to feel a little happier in her new role. She hadn't suffered the pangs of homesickness that she had thought might afflict her. Indeed, she had hardly thought about her papa, Mama Collins and her home at Longbourn since arriving at the castle.

She had written a letter to her father and stepmother, announcing her safe arrival, hoping that they and Harriet were well and asking that more of her clothes should be sent to her if possible.

Mrs Crawford had explained that letters left on a tray in the south hall would be sent on and that Catherine would not need to pay for their delivery, which was a blessing as she had very little money with her. She was beginning to realise that no one had ever told her whether she was to be employed as a governess and paid a salary, or live here as Matilda's companion for a few months as a guest of Sir Robert.

A deeper affection was beginning to grow between her and Matilda. The child still would not speak, but she seemed happier, and even Lady Honoria's occasional appearance in the drawing-room at tea-time did not quench her spirits.

But for all her enjoyment of her time spent with Matilda, Catherine had to admit that she did suffer a little from loneliness. Her evening meal, even though it was now served in the breakfast room, was often eaten alone. Sometimes Lady Honoria did favour her with her company and Catherine enjoyed those evenings a great deal. The old lady had travelled throughout Europe when young, had visited Florence and Rome and could describe all the wonders she had seen.

Nevertheless, quite often Catherine was on her own after Matilda had gone to bed and she wandered through the castle, or out into the nearby grounds, trying to decide if this way of life was any better than that she had had at Longbourn. She also found herself wishing, quite hard, that Sir Robert would return to Courtney.

5

The dry weather of early summer gave way to rain. It dawned wet and windy with dark clouds driving in from the sea. Catherine and Matilda had spent hours in the neglected flower garden, weeding and rescuing plants that were smothered in brambles. Their sketch books were full of roses in bud and opening out into full glory. Matilda had discovered a forgotten bird bath hidden under a bed of thistles and once she had carried water from the stables, sat for hours watching and waiting for the birds to arrive.

On Sundays, dressed neatly and soberly, they had accompanied Lady Honoria in the carriage to a church in a village two miles away inland. As befitted the Courtney standing in the neighbourhood, their pew was at the front of the church and Catherine tried her best to stop Matilda from wriggling through the long sermon.

At the door after the service, the vicar greeted Lady Honoria with great humility and respect: Catherine was reminded, against her will, of times in her childhood, when her dear papa had acted in an identical fashion towards his benefactor, Lady Catherine De Bourgh. She realised that in lots of ways Lady Honoria reminded her of her late benefactress. They were both proud women who put family before everything else: bearing that in mind, Catherine was still puzzled as to why her namesake had taken the trouble to make sure that her rector's daughter had a good education.

Now the warm weather had broken and, at breakfast on this wet day, Mrs Crawford announced that she had received a message from Sir Robert to say he was due home that morning; she told Catherine that he had added a promise to Matilda in his note that he would be there in time for luncheon and Catherine felt the little girl quiver in excitement when she heard those words.

They spent the next hours in the nursery, drawing in their sketch books pictures of birds, flowers, shells, mermaids and big fish. Catherine had unpacked the books she had borrowed from Bennetta's governess and stacked them on the bookcase. They would come in very handy when her own knowledge was exhausted.

She watched the little girl bent over her work; she was neat and tidy and had a talent for sketching, that was obvious. She was not a difficult child to teach or amuse but only their daily visits to the stables seemed to really rouse her interest - that and Bessie's night-time stories. Used to her half-sister's tempestuous character, Catherine found Matilda a sad little soul. No child should be this well-behaved. Apart from the early problems with porridge, there was no sign of the wild child that Sir Robert had described.

After luncheon the rain stopped, the clouds were driven away by a light breeze and the sun shone down on the castle. Sir Robert had not yet returned and Catherine found Matilda halfway down the turret stairway, staring out of an arrow slit window, obviously watching for her father to appear, cantering up the path towards the drawbridge.

There was something so forlorn and sad in her demeanour that Catherine found herself growing angry. Obviously, Sir Robert could not take his daughter with him, especially if he was visiting the lady he wanted to marry, but he had apparently promised to be home this morning and he had not kept his word. Perhaps the attractions of Miss Abigail Richmond had made him forget!

Catherine didn't know why she was so annoyed. Most fathers had little to do with their children until they were old enough to be out of the nursery and to partake in sensible conversation. She knew her own papa hardly saw Harriet except when she was brought into his study for him to read to her from the Bible. Catherine found herself smiling; those sessions were always cut very short by Harriett kicking the chair with both feet and grizzling in a very annoying fashion.

She had spent the last two weeks thinking about Sir Robert's obvious concern and love for Matilda, about his grief over her affliction. She had felt a growing sympathy for a man who controlled so much, was used to dealing with all sorts of problems, realising how difficult he must find it, not being able to do anything to overcome the biggest worry in his life. But perhaps she had been wrong to lavish so much thought and concern on a man who could not keep a promise.

Grimly, she decided to try and divert Matilda's attention from her father's lack of concern. What was needed was exercise and fresh air. Old dresses, bonnets, shawls and sturdy boots were found and donned and together they hurried out of the castle and down the sloping ground towards the seashore.

At the end of the promontory on which Courtney Castle stood, two paths zigzagged down the cliff face. Catherine peered over the edge of the one to the south, but even though the tide was out, there were wicked rocks below. To the north the path descended in shallow steps to a small cove which was hollowed out from the cliffs themselves. Sheltered from the worst of the weather, it looked calm and peaceful. There was a ripple of white sand and tiny rock pools that looked far more inviting than the ragged boulders on the other side of the promontory.

"Come, Matilda," she said, holding out her hand. "Let us explore along the beach." She laughed. "Why, we may even find the cavern made of emeralds that Bessie tells you stories about!"

The child's eyes gleamed and wisps of fair hair escaped from her pink bonnet as the wind gusted in. On the sand they were sheltered by the curve of the rocks and picked their way along the shoreline, jumping over the little waves that creamed onto the sand.

Suddenly a wave splashed a little higher, leaving a great stream of seaweed behind, shining with fat bladders of green and gold. Catherine picked up one end and began to run with the weed streaming behind her like a kite, her body light with the joy of living. She could hear Matilda laughing, a real sound. Then the child had caught the other end of the banner and together they danced round and round, giggling, their boots sinking into the damp sand, the bottom of Matilda's pantalettes and Catherine's skirt heavy with water and grit....

High above them two riders cantered gently along the cliff path. Reining in their mounts they sat gazing out to sea.

"It's a beautiful view, Sir Robert." Abigail Richmond smoothed down the skirt of her red velvet riding habit. Tall and handsome, with dark hair and grey eyes, she carried herself with all the confidence that came with being the spoilt only daughter of extremely rich, elderly parents. "I'm glad you persuaded me to ride with you rather than travel in the carriage with my maid and the luggage."

Her companion tried to smile: he had hoped to be back at the castle much earlier in the day. A promise had been made to Matilda that he would be there in time for luncheon but Abigail had taken such a time to get ready and even when they had left the carriage to the rough roads and galloped across country, she had wanted to stop often to admire the view.

He had told her that he had given his daughter his word to be home that morning, but Abigail had just laughed and teased him, saying that no one ever takes promises as binding, especially not the children. Sir

Robert was not sure but this was the woman he was thinking of marrying, so he knew he had to make allowances.

"Why you may be right. But listen, perhaps you can just call me Robert, as you did when we were children. We are such old friends."

Abigail raised an eyebrow. It was not the most gentlemanly of reminders of her age, that they had played together as children, but it was true. They had been a happy group, six youngsters growing up close to each other. The Courtneys and herself from families with land and money, Lucinda the daughter of a distinguished widowed gentleman who wrote serious books about historical battles in Ancient Greece and Persia. He travelled a great deal and his daughter had been left in the care of governesses and housekeepers. Mrs Richmond had gathered the little girl under her wing, and she had become an accepted member of the children's lives.

A spoilt only child who had been given everything she wanted in life, Abigail had never doubted that because she wanted it to happen, Robert would marry her when they grew up. One day he would inherit the title and she wanted to be Lady Courtney and live in the castle. And what Abigail wanted was all important to everyone in her world. Her merest wish, the slightest hint, had been granted immediately by her parents. She felt she had never quite recovered from the anger and despair she had endured when, at fifteen, her eyes were opened to the realisation that Robert only had one wife in view, their friend, Lucinda.

The fact that he didn't see what Lucinda was really like angered her even more. Men were in thrall to the fair hair, the slanting blue eyes, the willowy, elegant figure. They placed her on a pedestal and worshipped her from afar.

Abigail had known Lucinda since they were infants and knew that under the fairy like exterior was a wild child who used to run bare-foot over the moors and played with the fishermen's children, her skirts tucked up inside her pantalettes. It wasn't until Abigail's own mother had come to realise that their neighbour's little girl needed guidance that the wildness had been subdued and a calmer, dreamier Lucinda took her place. But Abigail knew it was just a facade. The other Lucinda had shown herself in the dare-devil horse-riding and carriage driving that had eventually cost her, her life.

But now....time had passed; Robert was surely over his grief and she was quite determined to be the next Lady Courtney. She didn't understand why he was being so slow in asking her. All their friends and neighbours expected an announcement daily! Obviously it could be nothing to do with her personally - she suspected that the problem was his unfortunate daughter.

Abigail pushed a strand of dark hair back under her hat. The child was a nuisance as she took up so much of Robert's time and thoughts, but once they were married...well, she had many poor elderly relations, living a long way from Courtney, who would be happy to have Matilda staying with them for a small fee..

She smiled sweetly. "You oblige me - Robert! I fear people are so free and easy with their manners these days." She laughed and nodded down towards the beach. "See that fisher woman and her child down there? Running around in the sand, playing with seaweed, probably soaking wet up to their knees. You must admit it is not the proper way to behave and a few years ago you would not have seen even a fisherman's wife do such a thing. I'm afraid standards have become very lax for all classes of society."

Sir Robert's mount snorted and bucked a little as the spurs that were hardly ever used, touched his side. His rider gazed down grimly at the little cove, trying to keep the expression of anger off his face: he had, at first, been reluctant to believe what he was seeing, but his eyesight was particularly good, and he was in no doubt that the child whose dress was now tucked up, showing her under garments was his daughter and the flying figure holding the other end of the seaweed banner was her new governess, Miss Catherine Collins!

As Catherine and Matilda walked back across the drawbridge and into the central courtyard, Matilda gave a sudden tug at Catherine's hand and darted off to where her father was standing, talking to one of the grooms.

Catherine felt her heart skip a beat. Sir Robert was looking directly over Matilda's head towards her, but his expression was anything but welcoming. She was horribly aware that Matilda's feet and pantalettes were soaked with sea water and that her own skirts were clinging to her legs, drenched in sand and grit.

Sir Robert ran his hand over his daughter's head, releasing the strings of her bonnet and letting her fair hair fly free. "It is good to see you, child. But you are very, very wet. Run upstairs immediately and find Bessie. We have an important visitor in the drawing-room and I am anxious that you make a good impression."

Catherine bent her head and tried to hurry past him up the steps after Matilda, but his voice rang out, stopping her. "Miss Collins! May I inquire why you and Matilda are so very wet and dirty when the afternoon has been dry and sunny?"

Raising her head, she stared into the dark blue eyes that could look so lovingly at the child but now were black and stormy as they gazed in her direction. She felt stung and irritated; he knew very well that they had been on the beach - where else would they have become so wet and sandy? He was playing games with her and she didn't care for it at all.

"As I am sure you can surmise, Sir, we have been down in the little cove at the bottom of the cliff steps. And yes, I am afraid we did get rather dirty, but then that is what happens when you are playing."

"But didn't I expressly command you not to put Matilda into any dangerous circumstances? In fact, I know I particularly mentioned the rocky shoreline. The tide can come in so fast that you can be swept away in seconds. I want to know why you disobeyed my instructions. Is this the way you mean to carry on, here at Courtney? If so - "

Catherine forgot that she was supposed to be calm and sensible. The inference that she was tardy in her guardianship stung her.

"I would never, ever put Matilda in danger! I was with her every second and we were not on the rocky shore, but on a sandy strip and no harm was likely to happen to us. She was becoming anxious when you did not return to Courtney this morning, as you promised, and I wanted to distract her."

There was an ominous silence. Catherine felt the blood drain away from her face; she had just been appallingly rude and he would have every right to send her away. But she refused to apologise. She was in the right and he was in the wrong. But sadly, from all she had experienced of gentlemen in the past, that didn't really matter.

She blinked back angry tears and jerked her chin higher. She would not cry in front of him. And to think that earlier she had felt sorry for the man, for his grief and his helplessness confronted by Matilda's affliction.

Sir Robert took a step forward in anger but what words he had been about to speak were lost as a woman's light, musical voice said, "Why Robert, I have long been changed and waiting for you. I ordered tea and it is getting cold. Is something the matter?"

Catherine and Sir Robert both turned to look at the woman who stood in the doorway on the steps above them, not knowing that they had identical expressions on their faces.

Abigail Richmond felt a stir of curiosity. It had been a very long time since she had seen Robert moved out of his usual grave demeanour, and it seemed very odd that this small, creature in a dirty, old-fashioned dress that clung to her legs could have caused it.

"Oh, I am sorry. Forgive me, I intrude. Should I retire?"

Sir Robert gave his dark head a quick shake. "No, of course not. I must apologise for delaying you. We were having a slight disagreement about Matilda."

"Oh, dear Matilda. I long to meet her again."

"And so you shall, very soon. She will be joining us in the drawing-room." He paused, took a deep breath and continued, "Let me introduce you - Miss Abigail Richmond, an old friend of the family, Miss Catherine Collins, companion and governess to Matilda and a family connection of my new sister-in-law, Cassandra."

Catherine curtseyed and Abigail nodded her head in acknowledgement. "I am delighted to meet you, Miss Collins. La, being a governess must be such an arduous task. I am sure I could never cope with all the lessons. My governess was such a strict old lady - do you remember, Miss Harrison, Robert? Always dressed in black and smelt of aniseed. We used to escape from her whenever we could, the poor old stick."

Catherine listened to the honeyed words and heard the slither of steel under them. So this was the woman Sir Robert was planning to marry. Dressed in the very latest fashion: tight-waisted, her long full sleeves of pale blue caught above and below the elbows with ribbons of lace, she was smiling sweetly but as far as Catherine was concerned, her grey eyes were as cold as the sea.

"Your poor governess had a lot to cope with. She was often asked to look after Lucinda, my brothers and sister and myself. I think a brace of governesses would have found it difficult to deal with six children as set on making mischief as we were."

Abigail laughed gently and walked gracefully down to their level. "Well, please do not let us keep you out here in the cold air, Miss Collins. I can see your dress is wet and your boots, too. You must not catch a chill, especially if you are taking care of dear Matilda."

"Yes, run along and get changed, Miss Collins. We shall continue this conversation at a later date." Sir Robert hesitated as he turned to escort Abigail up the steps. "Oh, and as you will not have had your tea, join us in the drawing-room when you are ready."

Catherine nodded, then felt her cheeks flush with colour as she heard Miss Richmond say as they walked indoors, "Oh dear, poor little soul. How kind you are to include her in a family gathering. She looks as if she would be far happier down in the fishing village, gutting herrings. Are you sure she is the right sort of person to have charge of Matilda?"

"Gutting herrings! Gutting herrings! What a rude woman." Catherine was angrily muttering under her breath as she picked up her skirts and hurried up the turret steps then along the corridor to her bedroom.

Pushing open the door to the nursery, she found the room empty. Matilda had gone downstairs already, and Catherine could only hope that Bessie had managed to get the dirt out from under the child's fingernails. Pulling off her own mud crusted gown, she knew she would be quite unable to appear as elegant and sophisticated as Miss Richmond.

"But why would you want to?" she murmured to herself as she found an afternoon dress that had once belonged to Bennetta. She held it up against herself and looked into the mirror. No! She would not try and pretend to be someone she was not.

In the closet she discovered an old dress of her own, simple and old-fashioned in green spotted muslin, it hung from a band of dark green brocade just under her breasts and was far more comfortable than the fashionable dresses with their corsets and petticoats. It was a little thin, but she had a warm shawl to wrap round her shoulders and at least the dress made her feel more at home. It was one her papa had liked to see her wearing, although she had to admit with a wry smile, that he would have been even prouder to have seen her decked out in all of Bennetta's cast off finery.

She stripped off her wet stockings and thrust her bare feet into her best green leather shoes to finish the outfit with a flourish. She was swirling a wet cloth over her face, hoping to banish any lingering sand and salt when there was knock on the door that led to the nursery and on her answering, Bessie Stokes appeared.

"I have taken Miss Matilda down to the drawing-room, Miss Collins."

"Thank you, Bessie. I must hurry there myself."

"Was wondering, Miss. My old Granma would dearly love to see the little Miss again. She is getting very old and may not be long for this world. Could you ask the Maister if it be all right for you to bring her along to my village one day?"

"Oh!" Catherine hesitated. Knowing how protective Sir Robert was of his daughter, she worried that a visit to a fishing village might not be something he would countenance. But then she recalled the child's fascination with Bessie's night time stories and remembered that Lucinda Courtney had taken her child to hear the tales so surely there could be no harm in a short visit?

"I can see no reason why not, Bessie," she said and was glad when the girl who was usually so sullen-faced, smiled. "And now I must run. I am very late for tea."

Picking up her shawl, she hurried to the turret stairway, her heart thumping. She was not looking forward to this social occasion. Surely Sir Robert would rather have Miss Richmond's company to himself? She couldn't imagine why he had asked her to attend; she could have taken tea up here in her room quite comfortably. Was he doing this just to annoy her, or to embarrass her in front of his lady friend?

As her thoughts grew more and more agitated, she spun faster and faster down the circular stairway. Then just as she reached the bottom turn, the leather sole on her shoe slid on the worn step and she was thrown forward, out into the hall and would have crashed down onto the stone floor if a man passing by had not automatically reached out to catch her in his arms.

"Oh! Oh, thank you!" Catherine gasped in confusion.

"Careful! You could have harmed yourself on this stone floor. Oh - why, why it's the dancing fairy girl from Pemberley! Whatever are you doing in Courtney Castle? Well, whatever, it is a delightful surprise. Yes, delightful!"

Warm hands held her shoulders, her shawl had fallen to the ground and she realised she had lost both her shoes in the accident. Catherine gazed up into bright green eyes that gleamed under a shock of blond hair. She was just about to pull herself away when a door nearby opened and she heard Sir Robert's voice, repeating the words he had spoken in the Pemberley gardens all those weeks ago.

"Let her go!"

6

Martin Courtney stretched out his long legs, smooth and heavily muscled in tight buff riding breeches, and cheerfully accepted a cup of hot chocolate from the footman. He glanced round the drawing-room, his eyes gleaming. Visits to his old home were usually very boring but necessary when funds ran low. He was fond of his big brother, but Robert had no time for society gossip and Martin was only able to feign interest in the workings of the Courtney estate for the very short time it took him to add a few precious guineas to his purse.

This visit, however, looked to be far more interesting. For a start, Abigail was staying at the castle, sitting across from him on another sofa, elegant in a pale blue dress of the very latest fashion. He rather thought she was only pretending to play with Matilda, dressing one of her dolls, because he could see her flicking little sideways glances at Robert next to her, lips curled in the smile of a doting mother. Rich, single, beautiful Abigail. Surely the next Lady Courtney.

For a few seconds Martin toyed idly with the idea of making love to Abigail, just to annoy Robert. It would be no great hardship; she was an attractive woman. In fact, he supposed that if he married her himself, then he wouldn't have to continually call on his brother for extra money to pay his London bills. But if he did that, then that would lessen Robert's chance of marrying and producing the vital heir that would stop him from inheriting the title in the event of his brother's death.

So, no, regretfully marrying Abigail was out of the question. His gaze flashed round the occupants of the drawing-room - Robert talking to Abigail but with a very odd expression on his face that Martin couldn't quite work out - irritation? - bewilderment? Neither was quite correct, but he was sure he would discover what was annoying his brother sooner or later.

He glanced at his Aunt Honoria, perched straight backed on the edge of her chair, her beady gaze darting round the round, sipping noisily from her cup and crumbling her shortbread petticoat tails all over her black satin skirt. And, on the other side of the room, the sprite of a girl in an old fashioned green muslin, pretending to nibble on a slice of bread and butter.

"So, Miss Collins, how do you find our northern climes? Harsher than your southern counties, of course. For example, dancing outdoors in the early dawn is not something that we often do for fear of catching a bad chill!"

Catherine felt hot colour flood her cheeks, well aware that he was referring to their first meeting in the Pemberley gardens, but managed to stay composed. "I like Northumberland very much, Sir."

"Miss Collins finds no difficulty in dancing anywhere, it seems to me." Robert's tone was harsh, his dark blue eyes stormy and Martin frowned. The girl had jumped as though bee stung. Now that was very interesting.

Catherine pinched her wrist through a fold in her dress. She would hold her tongue; she would not answer back, then heard herself saying, "Dancing is extremely good exercise for the mind and body, Sir. I intend to teach Matilda every dance I know, so she will be proficient in a few years' time when she attends balls and parties."

"Nothing wrong with dancing," Lady Honoria said. "Good at it myself. Used to be. Could dance all night and never feel tired. Young girls these days, no stamina."

"Miss Collins, do those dances include the one you were teaching her on the beach earlier?" Sir Robert asked getting up suddenly and walking across the room to stare out of the window.

"That was not a formal dance, Sir. Just an expression of our happiness at being outside in the fresh air."

Abigail smiled sweetly. "Robert, pray do not sound so censorious. The life of a governess, trying to pass on to a child whatever little knowledge she has, must be a very difficult one. I applaud Miss Collins for her dedication to Matilda. Surely you can forgive a little high-spirited behaviour?"

Sir Robert returned to the sofa and smiled down at her. "Abigail, you are quite right. I am being unnecessarily intolerant. I fear I sound as if I am criticising Miss Collins. I am not. We all have our own characters. It was just that I had made my preferences to Mrs Darcy quite clear. I wanted Matilda to have a companion whose first characteristic was common-sense."

"How incredibly boring!" Martin laughed and ran his fingers through his bright blond hair. He crossed the room, sank into a chair at Catherine's side and smiled warmly at her. "And do you prize common-sense as highly as my brother, Miss Collins? The only two previous times I have seen you, you have been bare footed and excited. Not very ladylike. How do you explain that away?"

Before Catherine could gather her wits to reply, Abigail's clear laughter rang through the room.

"Martin! Don't be such a tease. Miss Collins must know better than anyone here how difficult it is to appear ladylike at all times. If you are not brought up in those circles, it can be very trying to behave with decorum all the time. And I am sure Matilda will not suffer too much from having a companion whose likes and dislikes are on her level. Now - this is a doll, Matilda. Doll. Can you say doll? Why don't you try?"

She leant forward and patted Matilda on the cheek as she spoke and Catherine wondered if she was the only person who saw the child flinch away from the elegant white fingers, heavily laden with rings. She felt a flash of annoyance. Matilda couldn't or wouldn't speak; but she wasn't stupid.

Rising from her chair, she moved to stand in front of Sir Robert. "Sir, I fear that you are not at all happy with my position here at Courtney. I am very sorry if you feel you have been misled by my cousin in some way. I can assure you that I am not a frivolous person, although perhaps not as strict with Matilda as you would like me to be. But of course, I realise that we have no formal arrangement here. I am your guest, not your employee, and so I can leave immediately if you would prefer."

Sir Robert stared up at the girl in front of him. He didn't know why she irritated him so much. Her life looking after her small sister had surely been boring and staid. She was the daughter of a country parson with a distant connection to a family of distinction. But surely she had nothing of any consequence to look forward to in the future. She should have been quiet and solemn and slightly in awe of him. Instead, she reminded him irresistibly of one of the small seabirds that flung themselves into the wind and skimmed above the waves of the restless sea outside. He was about to speak, then he frowned. The girl's lips were quivering! Did she dare laugh at him?

"Matilda! Come over here, child. That is a new doll, I do believe. Let me inspect her."

Lady Honoria had no time for small children or this modern habit of them taking tea with the adult members of the family, but she had noticed that the little girl was now standing behind her father, pulling faces at Miss Collins over his shoulder, trying to make her laugh. It was the first sign of normal childish naughtiness that she had seen from Matilda in two years and for a second tears stung her eyes.

"Do you play the piano, Miss Collins?" Abigail asked suddenly. "Perhaps you would favour us."

"My skills are very poor, Miss Richmond. Little tunes for children, country dancing and a few hymns. I would never inflict my efforts on company."

"Oh, how I do miss the musical evenings we used to have at Courtney Hall. Lucinda played the piano so beautifully." She walked across the room and stood gazing up at the portrait above the fireplace. "But then she was all elegance and accomplishment. We must hope that Matilda inherits those qualities. But she will need someone to teach her just how a lady should act."

Martin had seated himself at the piano and was playing a lively march. "Elegance and beauty and accomplishment - what more could a man want in a wife? Don't you agree, Robert?"

"Lucinda was a devoted wife and mother. I found no fault in her."

"Oh, I so agree," Abigail cried, clasping her hands in front of her as if in prayer. "Her memory will always be honoured by all who knew her."

"But life must go on." Lady Honoria broke into the conversation, her voice harsh. "It always does. If Miss Collins won't play for us, perhaps you will yourself Abigail? Anything to stop young Martin ruining the keyboard with his heavy touch."

There was a moment's silence and then Abigail said, regretfully, "Alas, I cannot today. My finger was caught under the bridle strap on the way here and was sadly twisted. But as soon as it recovers, I will be only too happy to lighten our evenings together."

Martin grinned to himself. It was quite obvious that with thoughts of Lucinda so clear in Robert's mind, Abigail was quite determined not to have her musical talents compared in any way.

"Ring the bell for Crawford," his aunt said suddenly. "I am sure Matilda has had enough of our company and will be happier back in her nursery."

Catherine did as she was bid and when Mrs Crawford appeared, Matilda was given into her care and sent upstairs to her nursery to play before supper.

Catherine was about to follow her when she hesitated. "Sir Robert, now that Matilda is no longer present, as horse-riding has been mentioned in the conversation, I am wondering, if this would be an appropriate time to ask about acquiring a pony for her. She is so very fond of horses and a little one of her own would be a delight for her."

"A pony?" Sir Robert looked at her, frowning.

"Yes, Sir. Just a small one. I can ride and once one of the grooms has taught her, I will be happy to accompany her along the tracks around the castle, if you wish me to remain as her governess, of course."

"Sounds like an excellent plan to me." Martin pushed another log onto the fire, ignoring his aunt's frown. He knew she expected him to ring for the footman to undertake such a task but the early summer air was chilly within the castle's stone walls.

"Oh, Miss Collins, please think what you are saying!" Abigail turned to Sir Robert, her eyes wide in entreaty. "How dangerous even a small pony might be, especially to a child who cannot talk and so can give no verbal instructions. No, no, I beg of you, Robert. Do not countenance such a worrisome scheme. Miss Collins must realise that Matilda is a very special child, delicate like her dear mama. She has not had a rough upbringing, such as perhaps her own, and might not survive another accident."

Catherine bit her lip. She would have loved to have made a sharp reply, to insist that her own upbringing, far from being robust, had been mostly spent under the watchful eye of a certain Lady Catherine de Bourgh of Rosings who had insisted that Mr and Mrs Collins' daughter be taught the very best of manners. Although her own daughter, the invalid Lady Anne, had had no success in instilling musical talent into Catherine, learning to ride under the strict instructions of the Rosings head groom had been a skill she had acquired quite easily.

But she knew she could not start a discussion with Abigail Richmond as to how Matilda should be educated. It was not her place. Abigail was probably about to become the next Lady Courtney and Matilda's step-mother. What she decreed is what would surely happen because Catherine could tell Sir Robert was only too willing to do everything to make his lady friend happy.

"I will give the matter some thought," Sir Robert said. "I know everyone has Matilda's best interests at heart, but I must admit to a great feeling of trepidation when I see her in the stables, walking so nonchalantly amongst animals that could fell her with one strike of their hooves."

A silence fell and everyone in the room knew that his mind had gone back to the terrible crash that had killed his wife. That he was picturing a horse rearing, hooves flailing in the air. Catherine felt a surge of pity sweep over her, but at the same time she felt it was wrong to deprive Matilda of something that she would so obviously enjoy just because of fears engendered by the past.

Martin jumped to his feet, determined to break the sombre mood. "Come, we must not be gloomy. Aunt Honoria, I'm sure you could entertain us with scandalous tales about your time spent in France. You must have been a beautiful young woman! I imagine duels were fought over you."

Lady Honoria turned her beady gaze on her nephew and Catherine was suddenly aware that the old lady's hands were trembling as she stroked the great ruby ring she wore. Whatever her memories were of that time in her life, when revolution had destroyed the French monarchy, they were obviously not pleasant ones and she felt a flash of anger at Martin for stirring up old emotions.

"Well, perhaps, perhaps... I am feeling very tired. Robert - I will not dine with you tonight. Please arrange for my meal to be served to me in my room. Miss Collins, your arm if you please. I intend to retire. I will bid you good day, Abigail...Martin...Robert."

Catherine hurried to offer her arm as the old lady got to her feet and with the briefest of nods, left the drawing-room. She said nothing as they made their way across the hall and down a passageway that led into the north hall where a wide staircase on the far side swept upwards in easy rising steps.

At the foot of the stairs Lady Honoria stopped, resting with both her hands on her cane, and gazed upwards into the gloom, as if the effort to ascend the stairway was too much.

"Will you rest, Madam?" Catherine asked anxiously. "I can bring a chair."

"Nothing wrong with my legs, child. Just my balance and my temper. I shouldn't get upset by stupidity, but then Martin was never the most understanding of children. All glister and no gold - mind you remember what Shakespeare said."

Mystified, Catherine murmured that she would.

Just then Mrs Crawford appeared and hurried towards them.

"Ah Crawford, yes, I have decided to eat in my room tonight. The company does not please me. If you will kindly give me your arm, I can release this young woman to go about her duties." She leant on the housekeeper's arm and made her way slowly up the stairs.

Catherine watched her, apprehensively: the old lady looked very frail. Footsteps sounded behind her and she turned to find Sir Robert.

"My aunt has reached a great age." He watched the old lady out of sight then leant against the carved newel post, frowning.

"She's an extremely interesting person," Catherine said. "But somehow sad. Has she had a very unhappy life?"

"I think it has been one of two halves. Come, let me show you." With a gesture, he beckoned her back along the passage way into the south hall and into his study. Confused, she followed him, aware that the two shaggy dogs were accompanying them everywhere they went.

Sir Robert opened a cabinet and took out a box painted in bright colours with panels of mystical animals. With great care he undid it and took out two miniatures, linked together by a thin gold chain, exquisitely painted in great detail. One showed the head and shoulders of a girl with a lot of dark hair, dressed high on her head in an old-fashioned style, little pearl droplets shining in the tresses. She wasn't particularly pretty but Catherine could see a likeness to the man standing next to her in the dark hair.

The other side of the portrait frame depicted a young man with a haughty expression. He was handsome but looked very grand and aristocratic, not the sort of man you would ever talk to easily, she thought.

"My aunt and her husband, Count Pierre du Bois. This was the only item she brought with her when she fled from Paris during the Revolution. When she arrived at Courtney after the death of my mother, she gave it to my father and bade him destroy it. But he saved it and now it has come down to me."

Catherine reached out to touch the frame and jerked her hand away as her fingers touched his. The sudden warmth sent a shock through her body. "Did he die in the Revolution?" she whispered at last.

Sir Robert sat down at his desk as if suddenly very tired. "Indeed. I am sure I don't need to tell you how. From what my father told me, Pierre du Bois was a hard-nosed aristocrat, who had no time for the poor who worked for him on his estate. My aunt married him when she was in her teens and would have died with him except that she believed she was carrying a child and headed for England and home so the du Bois line would continue."

Catherine sank down onto a chair next to him, still holding the miniature. "But..." she stopped.

"But there was to be no child, no heir and, of course, after the Revolution, there was no estate or house for her to return to in France."

"How very sad." Catherine found her eyes full of tears. She gazed again at the portraits - two young people whom life would tear apart. "She must have been very brave. I will hope to impart some of her story to Matilda. I am sure you would wish her to be just as brave." There was no reply, so she went on, valiantly, "So France was just the first part of your aunt's life?"

Sir Robert gave a start, as if he had been thinking of something else. "Yes, caring for us was the second. Four children running wild after our mother died. Our father was too taken up by grief to give us a moment's consideration. I am ashamed to say we were having a wonderful time, doing exactly what we liked, when we liked. Then Aunt Honoria arrived and life settled down. She soon taught us our manners and curbed our more outlandish behaviour! But we grew to love her. Martin is too careless in what he says. He knows she does not like to be reminded of Pierre and that dreadful time in France."

"So perhaps as she had no children of her own, the second part of her life, caring for her niece and nephews was happy?"

Sir Robert looked at her intently, then he gently removed the miniature from her hand and took it across to the cabinet. "Is loving someone else's children easy?"

Catherine saw his frown and guessed he was thinking of Abigail and Matilda. "Oh yes, I am sure if you love someone, then you would find it quite easy to love whom they love."

Sir Robert's dark blue eyes looked almost black as he gazed down at the small girl perched on the edge of her chair like a little green bird. He could see the glints of bright brown hair on the back of her neck that had escaped from the strict braid that strained upwards to coil around her ears.

He was going to reply, then stopped himself. It would not be appropriate to enter into a conversation about love with this girl who was more than ten years younger than him. He sifted through the box with gentle fingers.

"I have all of my wife's jewellery in here for Matilda when she is old enough. She likes to play dress up with it. She has Lucinda's miniature by her bedside but I wonder if she is already forgetting her face."

"I have seen the portrait there. It is very beautiful. I do believe it is Matilda's prize possession. Surely with that before her she will not forget her mother?"

"I hope so, but a year or two is a long time for a little girl and I worry that remembering her mama will also bring back memories of the accident and make her even less likely to speak."

He shut the cabinet with a decisive bang and remarked stiffly that he must return to his guest and that he was sure Matilda would be awaiting Catherine upstairs.

She nodded, startled at his ending their talk so abruptly, but as she made her way back across the hall and up the spiral stairway, she was remembering the touch of his fingers on hers and wondered how poor Lady Honoria had survived losing in that dreadful fashion someone she loved so dearly.

Back in the drawing-room, Martin had seated himself at the piano again and was playing a tune with one finger. He looked up as Abigail came to stand next to him, leaning elegantly against his shoulder. "So, my dear, when can I expect to welcome my new sister-in-law into the family?"

She pouted. "Oh, give me a few more days, Martin. He seems to be on the verge of asking and then something or someone interrupts us."

"You don't love him."

"Really, Martin! That is not the sort of statement you should make to the woman who will shortly be your sister-in-law."

"Abigail, we have known each other since you were in pantalettes and I was in a smock! I've always known you wanted to marry Robert; it was just a pity that he thought he was in love with Lucinda. But wanting to marry someone isn't the same as loving them."

"Robert and I will be perfectly happy together. He needs a wife, a hostess to help him fulfill his role as the prominent landowner of the district."

Martin played a loud discord on the keyboard. "And what benefit do you gain from the match, pray?"

Abigail moved to the fireplace but resolutely refused to look up at Lucinda's portrait. When she ruled here at Courtney, that would be one picture that would be discreetly retired to an upstairs landing. She wasn't quite certain how to answer Martin. She wanted to be Lady Courtney, that was true, but it was more than that. She had to wipe out the feeling of being over-looked, of not getting what she wanted. And most of all she wanted Robert to desire her in the way she desired him.

Before she could speak, the door opened and the man in question entered, making some apology about taking care of his aunt.

"Robert! Martin and I have just decided that what we need is some entertainment. I believe you promised that I might organize a dinner party whilst I am here." She held out her hands, laughing, all pretty entreaty. In her imagination she could see herself standing next to him, greeting his guests as they arrived, making the perfect couple. He would see then that he could not do without her. Surely then he would propose.

"Did I?"

"Why not?" Martin took up her cause. "You are getting old and staid, brother. A large dinner party to entertain your friends and family in honour of Abigail's visit will be delightful. With enough couples, we could even open the ballroom and have some dancing."

And, he thought dryly, if you can't see that she is arranging that to be the perfect occasion for you to propose, then your knowledge of women and their wiles is sadly lacking. He smiled to himself. This visit to Courtney was becoming more interesting with every passing hour. He was looking forward to the dinner party and found himself deciding that he would have one or more dances with Miss Catherine Collins.

7

The next morning Catherine woke to brilliant sunshine streaming in through her window. She washed and dressed and peered out at blue cloudless skies and a flat silken sea. She intended to spend all day outside if possible, far away from Abigail Richmond. There was something about that lady that dampened even the highest spirits. A tap on the door and Bessie and Matilda entered.

"Good morning, Bessie. A lovely day. And good morning to you, Matilda. You look very pretty today." She reached out to stroke the girl's long fair hair.

"Yes, Miss. That's just what I was a saying to Miss Matilda."

"I haven't forgotten what you asked of me, Bessie. I shall put your request to Sir Robert this morning. As it is so fine, today would indeed be perfect for a walk along the cliff path towards your village. I realise it is not your half day off, but perhaps, with Mrs Crawford's permission, you would not be averse to accompanying me and Matilda?"

Bessie's green eyes gleamed. "I'd be happy to. My old granma will be right pleased to see the little maid again."

Catherine spun her long braids up around her head and searched for hair pins to keep them fastened. Bessie gently pushed her hands away and took over the fixing herself. She was far quicker, and more deft, and Catherine had to admit that her hair looked far neater and pulled less at the skin around her temples.

"I hear there's to be a dinner party with dancing, Miss."

"Really?" Catherine was disconcerted. This must have been arranged the night before. She had had no wish to go back downstairs after Matilda had gone to bed and had asked Mrs Crawford for her meal to be served in her room.

"That Miss Richmond has told the Master she would like to have one. Been a long time since the castle saw such an event. The old ballroom is to be opened up and aired, although I wonder what state it will be in. Running with mice and spiders, I daresay, but just think, a dance here at Courtney!"

"It sounds very exciting." She turned to Matilda. "I think a party means a new dress for you, Matilda. I am sure your papa will want to show you off to his guests before you go to bed."

The little girl looked up at her, eyes wide and for a second Catherine saw her lips form a word and, thrilled, thought she was about to speak. But the moment passed and she just tugged at Catherine's hand, eager to go downstairs for her breakfast.

She was more than surprised when they entered the room to find Sir Robert, Martin and Abigail already seated at the table. Matilda ran to her father for a good morning kiss and Catherine blushed as Martin leapt to his feet to hold out a chair next to his own. Abigail, resplendent in a pale lemon morning dress, yawned, nodded once and bent her head over her toast and honey.

"Good morning, Miss Collins. I trust you slept well. I was sorry not to see you at dinner last night." Martin was all solicitude, his fingers warm on her arm as he helped her to her seat.

"Thank you, Sir. I admit I was a little tired but am quite refreshed this morning."

"Good morning, Matilda...Miss Collins." Sir Robert was finishing a plate of cold roast beef. "I, too, was sorry you did not join us for dinner last night. As you are aware, in my absence it has been arranged that dinner will be served in the breakfast room! Well, to be fair, the food was hot and inviting."

Abigail looked up, frowning, then smiled. "Robert told us that you suggested the alteration, Miss Collins. Such a good idea. It is always useful to have someone close to the family who is versed in household affairs. I'm afraid my parents would never have deemed it a suitable accomplishment for me to obtain."

There was a silence. Sir Robert pushed his plate away, rubbed his hand across his dark hair and addressed Catherine. "What are your plans for today?"

Catherine helped herself to bread and a slice of ham. A footman had already placed the usual hated bowl of porridge in front of Matilda and the little girl was busy making paths of honey across the surface.

"An outing for which I would need your permission, Sir."

"Oh?"

"I would like to take Matilda to visit the nursery maid Bessie Stoke's grandmother. Apparently she is extremely old and..." she glanced at Matilda and said softly..."well, extremely old and would be honoured to see the child before..well....before..."

"I remember old Granny Stokes!" Martin broke in, holding up his cup to be refilled. "So do you, Robert and you, Abigail. She lives in a tiny hovel in the next village north along the coast." He laughed. "Everyone said she was a witch and don't you recall, Lucinda used to dare us to knock on her door and run away."

"I'm sure I did no such thing," Abigail said crossly. "Really, Martin. What a thing to say in front of Matilda. Granny Stokes was a dirty old crone and we were supposed to keep away from her in case we caught some dreadful disease. I'm sure she will not have improved and I certainly can see no reason for her to have a visit from Miss Matilda Courtney!"

"But when we were married, Lucinda used to take Matilda to explore the fishing villages," Sir Robert said quietly. "That was why she took on Mrs Stokes' granddaughter, Bessie, to be Matilda's nursery maid when she was born."

"So, do I have permission to take Matilda this morning? And to approach Mrs Crawford and ask for Bessie to accompany us. It is a lovely day for a walk along the cliffs."

"Yes - and I shall join you!" Martin raised his coffee cup in a mocking toast. "I think I can protect a beautiful young lady from the dangerous Granny Stokes." His laughter was aimed towards Matilda and then, under his breath he said to Catherine, "Two beautiful young ladies!"

She felt the hot colour rush up into her cheeks and bent her gaze to her plate. She knew Martin Courtney was playing at being a flirt, but it still raised her spirits to have a man look at her with admiration.

"Martin! You have surely not forgotten that you promised to help me write invitations for the dinner party this morning?" Abigail sounded less than pleased. "I can appreciate that you feel Miss Collins might not be up to the task of protecting dear Matilda from sights and sounds she really should not be exposed to, but surely one of the footmen could go in your place?"

"My dear Abigail, we only decided on the dinner last night. Surely any plans can wait a day or two?"

Sir Robert scrunched up his napkin and threw it onto the table. "No, Abigail is quite right. If there is to be a social event here at Courtney Castle, then it needs to be properly planned."

His guest smiled warmly at him. "Thank you, Robert. I knew I could rely on you."

"Yes, Martin must stay and help in any way you choose. I will escort Matilda and Miss Collins myself."

The look of displeasure that crossed Abigail's face was fleeting as she clapped her hands together as if in delight. "Oh, on second thoughts, it is too nice a day to be spent indoors, writing out invites. We can do them this evening. Why don't we all go? I will ask Mrs Crawford to arrange a picnic basket. It will be a wonderful outing."

"Oh what joy - sitting on damp grass with buzzing insects all around. What a way to spend a morning!" Martin smiled at Catherine. "But then, as I am sure you are really a sprite of the woods, you will feel quite at home, Miss Collins."

"Martin!" Sir Robert's voice was sharp and Catherine wondered why he let his brother disturb him so much. He must know it was just teasing and silliness. She was not at all offended by the casual remarks.

"Well, it seems to be settled," Sir Robert continued. "Perhaps you will confer with Mrs Crawford, Abigail, and I will arrange for a carriage. Miss Collins, if you have finished your meal, perhaps you would kindly take Matilda upstairs before she becomes completely stuck to the table with honey and find her some more suitable clothes for an outing in the countryside. Nothing too fancy or that will be ruined if it should get dirty."

Fifteen minutes later, Catherine had just dispatched an excited Matilda and an even more excited Bessie downstairs to await the carriage when a tap at the door brought Mrs Crawford.

"Goodness, Miss Collins, what a to do. There's cook lamenting her lunch that will now be ruined and having to find cold meats and tartlets for a picnic, and that Miss Richmond giving orders left and right about getting the castle ready for a dance, till I don't know if I am coming or going."

Catherine smiled. "Well, it is very acceptable to have a change from our normal routine, isn't it? And Matilda is excited at seeing Bessie's grandmother again."

Mrs Crawford sniffed. "That's as maybe - how you can tell when she can't speak, I'm sure I don't know. But in the meantime, I have a message from the Master. He says if you have a heavy skirt and boots, will you please wear them."

"A thick skirt?" Catherine stared out of the window at the bright sunshine. "Surely it is too warm?" As the cliff walk was obviously not going to happen, she had changed into one of Bennetta's treasured dresses, a red-spotted muslin, that although not as elegant as anything Abigail might wear, was none the less of good quality and suited her colouring. She had even found a length of bright red ribbon that she had tied round her straw hat.

"Aye, you may well sound bemused. But he's probably thinking that some of these fishermens' cottages can only be reached by rough tracks and thin shoes will be destroyed on the rocks."

Catherine nodded and when the housekeeper had left, rapidly changed. Casting the muslin onto her bed, she pulled out her heavy dark blue skirt and jacket She had not worn them since her journey to Northumberland and they were sadly crumpled, but they were the only garments she had that sounded correct.

Down in the stable courtyard all was confusion. The pony and trap was waiting with young Donald handling the reins, the shaggy pony stamping his hoof, impatient to be off. Bessie and Matilda were already sitting in the trap, with two large picnic baskets strapped on behind them.

A splendid open carriage enameled in darkest blue with the Courtney crest emblazoned on the sides was harnessed and ready, a groom standing at the horses' heads, holding their bridles. Already on board, Martin was sitting laughing at Abigail who had, Catherine noticed, changed from her lemon morning dress to an elegant affair in cream lace with wide, full sleeves of the palest gold, caught above and below her elbows with dark golden ribbons. Her parasol was of gold lace and threw pretty shadows across her face.

In her heavy blue serge skirt and jacket, Catherine stood in the castle doorway, feeling hot and uncomfortable. She stared unhappily at the carriage. She would have to sit next to Abigail - there was no room in the pony-trap. Bewildered, she realised she didn't understand Sir Robert. Was he trying to make it clear, by ordering what she wore, that she must recognise her position at the castle?

"What is Miss Collins wearing? Such a sight! Surely the girl has a more suitable outfit for a summer picnic?" Abigail's clear, high voice carried across the yard.

Catherine saw Martin turn and frown across at her and suddenly a wave of anger swept over her. She was Miss Catherine Collins of Longbourn and would not be treated so disdainfully. She pulled on her summer hat, tied the frivolous red ribbon under her chin with a flourish and marched across the yard towards the carriage.

What she would have said, she was never to know because just then, the stable doors opened and Sir Robert rode out on his big bay hunter, and trotting at his side on a leading rein was a smaller grey mare with a silvery mane and tail.

Catherine watched in astonishment as he wheeled both horses round to face her.

"Ah, Miss Collins. I see you got my message about a heavy skirt. I wondered if you had a riding habit with you and then decided that you probably did not. I thought as you had suggested riding at some time in the future with Matilda, this would be a good opportunity for me to ascertain how proficient you are."

"Oh!" Catherine didn't know if she was pleased, scared or annoyed. This obviously meant he expected her to stay at Courtney, that she was forgiven for being impertinent. She reached out and patted the silky grey neck.

"The mare is quiet and reliable. I am not expecting you to jump hedges and ditches to show me your prowess; just that I can trust you will be able to care for Matilda if I do decide to buy her a pony in the distant future. Of course, it is quite understood that even if I do, you will never ride out without a groom accompanying you."

"Really, Robert, what a time to interrogate poor Miss Collins." Abigail did not sound pleased, although Catherine could see from the sparkle in Matilda's eyes that she had understood every word and all that it implied.

"Well, I think it's a good plan." Martin lay back indolently. He gestured to the groom holding the carriage horses steady. "Right, Biggs, let's see how far we can get before they catch us up."

As Catherine watched, the carriage and pony trap lurched into motion and vanished in a cloud of dust through the archway and out onto the cliff path. Then Sir Robert was swinging down from his horse and coming to stand by her side.

"Are you ready to ride, Miss Collins?"

She could hear a challenge in his voice. Did he think she would simper and say no, she couldn't possibly ride a horse she knew nothing about? Did he expect her to stay here at the castle whilst he rode out after the others for their picnic?

Without answering, she took hold of the mare's reins and glanced round for a mounting block. Before one of the stable-hands could walk forward to help her, Sir Robert had taken her foot in his hand and with one swift movement threw her up into the saddle.

Gasping, she settled herself as the mare shifted at the sudden weight, curling her knee round the saddle horn and pushing her heavy skirt down over her petticoats. A riding habit would have been useful, but the thick material was protecting her from leather and buckles.

Sir Robert gazed up at her. She had been as light as a feather in his hands, submitting to his efforts without any feminine squeals of protest. Now she was turning the mare as he mounted his horse once more. “I see you know how to handle her, Miss Collins.”

Catherine nodded, suddenly delighting at being on horseback once more. “It is quite a long time since I rode a good horse, Sir,” she said as they walked their mounts out of the stable yard. “We only have two elderly carriage horses at home in Longbourn. They both object to a saddle and bridle.”

She didn’t feel it necessary to tell him that Lady Catherine de Bourgh had felt that riding should be amongst her accomplishments. She had never understood why that terrifying old lady had taken such a liking to her parson’s child. Perhaps it had been because she had never been afraid of her, never scared of her sharp tongue, had seen that behind her autocratic manner was an extremely unhappy woman.

As she grew older, she had realised that both her dear Mama and Papa were always anxious in the echoing halls and cavernous rooms of the great house of Rosings. They became people she hardly recognised and it had puzzled her a great deal.

A sudden memory flashed into her mind - Lady Anne had been playing the piano for her one afternoon and she had been dancing round the vast music room. Lady Anne had been laughing - as thin and frail as she was it was rare to hear her laugh. Now Catherine could remember Lady de Bourgh standing in the doorway, watching and listening with an expression on her face that was a mixture of sadness that her daughter would never dance and delight that something had given her pleasure and made her laugh.

By now she and Sir Robert had ridden out from the castle and along the cliff path. A cloud of dust ahead of them showed where the carriage had passed by.

"Lord, we will be choked following in their wake," he said. "Are you game to try your mount across country, Miss Collins? We can head up that hill ahead of us. It is not difficult ground."

Without waiting to reply, Catherine kicked the mare forward into a canter and, leaving her companion behind, set off up the rough grassy slope, urging her mare on, delighting to feel all her old skills in the saddle returning. The wind stung her face and she laughed in delight at the wonderful feeling of freedom.

With a gasp she felt the red ribbon on her hat slip and it cartwheeled from her head. At the top of the hill, she reined the mare to a halt and turned to find Sir Robert cantering slowly up behind her, her straw hat clutched in one hand, the red ribbons had vanished but the straw seemed undamaged.

"Bravo, Miss Collins. Bravo! Bravely ridden. And this is yours, I believe."

Catherine took it, laughing. She was aware that her carefully braided hair had not survived her headlong gallop and was beginning to unwind down her back. Their fingers met as he handed her the hat and the laughter died from her lips as, for a second, the world seemed to tilt and she felt a wave of dizziness sweep over her. His dark blue eyes seemed to hold her gaze and he was smiling in a way she had never seen before.

Without a word, he pointed to the east and she turned and gasped. She could see for miles. The whole of the Northumberland coastline lay before them, wide stretches of sand, rocky coves and cliffs. Today the sea was calm and blue, gulls screaming as they floated in the wind, the grass rippling under the horses' hooves. It was lonely and wonderful and beautiful; they could have been the only two people left alive in the world and she turned to smile at Sir Robert in a moment of shared delight.

He dismounted and held out his arms for her to slide down to the ground. She tried not to flinch at his touch - it was no more personal than that of a groom. They stood together, the horses snuffling at the thin grass, then Sir Robert turned and pointed away from the sea, inland. The land rose in a series of low hills and moorland, dotted with sheep. All was blue and green and glorious in the early summer sun, but Catherine could imagine that it would look very bleak and unfriendly once the snows came.

"All this is part of the Courtney estate," Sir Robert said, and she could tell from the warmth in his voice that he loved every acre of it.

At that moment he reminded her of Mr Darcy - a quiet man who did not show his feelings lightly but had a passionate love for the land under his control.

"My father was a good man but adverse to modern methods and he was ill for a long time, refusing to pass over control of the estate to me."

He turned back to look out to sea. "Courtney is responsible for two coal mines and several of the little fishing villages as well. The one we are about to visit is such. Times are hard; fishing is a precarious business, many drown at sea. I'm well aware that there might even be some smuggling in the district, but I turn a blind eye, although the authorities would not be pleased to know that! But the fishermen have to put food on their tables and roofs over their heads. You will see that some of the cottages are in bad repair, but believe me, Miss Collins, I am well aware of the situation and doing all in my power to rectify matters although the income from the estate is very low."

"It can't be easy," Catherine said quietly.

"No - Richard never cared overmuch for the land and Martin just wants a carefree life. But I cannot walk away. If I do not have a son in the future, then Martin will inherit on my death and if, by chance, we both perish in some plague, then Richard and Cassandra will live here. But whatever Fate holds in store, I must garner together a good fortune to leave to Matilda."

Catherine reached out to stroke her mare's silky neck. If Sir Robert was talking about a son, then surely marriage to Miss Richmond must be on his mind and likely to happen very soon. And she could well imagine that Abigail would bring a large sum of money into the marriage - money that Sir Robert needed desperately to keep the Courtney estate in a healthy state. She sighed; at every turn it seemed that he would be most unwise not to propose to that lady!

"The estate is not yours to dispose of as you see fit, Sir?"

He turned his dark blue gaze on her face, noticing the fine colour that the wind had whipped into her cheeks. "No, it is not. It passes to the oldest male child. If my brothers and sister or I have no male heir, then it passes to a very distant cousin who resides in Italy and whom I have never met."

His grave expression lightened for a second and his eyes twinkled. "You can see that I already await news from Richard and Cassandra of a happy event with great hope!"

Catherine smiled. "I am sure such news would delight everyone." She hesitated then went on; "My father inherited our present house when Cousin Elizabeth's father died. It was entailed away from the Bennets. I believe it caused a great deal of anguish before all the Bennet girls were married."

Sir Robert helped her back into her saddle and she took a moment to push her hair back up under her sun hat, regretting the loss of her ribbons, as he mounted his own horse and took a final look out at the view.

"It can be a very hard life here in the winter," he said softly, almost as if he was talking to himself. "The snows can be heavy; the castle can be cut off from the outside world for days on end. Entertainment and society are in short supply, even on a fine day such as today. It is not an easy life to ask someone to share."

He thought of Abigail; she had grown up locally, that was true, but he also knew that she adored the society of York and Edinburgh, the excitement of London, the elegance of Bath. But, of course, she was the right choice for him. He had no idea why he was prevaricating in proposing marriage to her.

Catherine was silent: she had no idea how to reply. Did he want her to say that Abigail would make the ideal chatelaine for Courtney Castle? Then the moment passed. She urged the mare into a walk and trotted down the hill path with Sir Robert at her side. He was silent and she felt confused, desperate to speak, to break the silence that lay between them but unable to think of a single thing to say.

They had just reached a smooth stretch of turf at the foot of the hill when a loud halloo sounded and there was Martin, walking up the path towards them, slim and elegant, hat in hand, his bright hair gleaming in the sunshine.

"I am delighted to see you have arrived in one piece, Miss Collins," he said, smiling warmly at her. "We were most disturbed to discover you were not following us along the track. Robert - your presence is desired most earnestly by Abigail. We have apparently found two perfect places for our picnic and only you must have the deciding vote."

"Certainly." Sir Robert said abruptly and urged his horse forward into a canter that took him away down the path at speed.

"May I escort you, Miss Collins? Pray, let me help you down. You will be tired if you have not ridden for some time."

Catherine let herself slip from the saddle and felt his hands around her waist, holding her just a little too long for comfort. She eased herself away and struggled to find her footing on the slippery path.

"It seems my brother cannot wait to get back to Abigail's side," Martin said as they walked slowly round a wide corner and, in the distance, they could see the little group sitting on the ground, the carriage nearby, the coachman and Donald caring for the horses.

"Indeed," Catherine murmured, feeling suddenly very foolish. "I am sorry if I have kept them apart. It was not my idea to ride across country, but your brother was annoyed by the dust the carriage disturbed."

She felt a flicker of anger. Sir Robert need not have made it quite so plain that he was keen to leave her company and join his great friend. She had thought from his expression that he had enjoyed their ride as much as she had. But she had been wrong.

Martin gazed down at the straw hat that came just to his shoulder. He had seen his brother's face as the two riders had come close to him and a very strange idea had begun to blossom in his mind. One that he needed time to think about because if he was right, then life at Courtney Castle was going to be even more interesting than he had possibly hoped.

8

When Catherine and Martin reached the picnic area, Sir Robert was sitting on the ground close to Abigail, helping her unpack the luxuries from the baskets, laughing at some comment she had whispered to him. Bessie was pouring lemonade for everyone. Martin handed the horses over to Donald and threw himself down on the rugs that had been strewn on the ground and accepted a glass of lemonade with cries of delight.

Now she had dismounted, Catherine realised how hot she was. The sun was beating down and the picnic had been laid in a natural hollow between two grassy slopes, out of any cooling sea breeze. The heavy skirt and jacket that had been so useful when riding now clung to her and she was mortified to find a trickle of perspiration running down her neck.

Matilda jumped up and ran across the grass to her, reaching for her hand and gazing up at her with a smile.

Sir Robert looked up briefly and nodded, his face oddly blank of all emotion. “You did well, Miss Collins. You have been taught to ride by an expert, I imagine.”

"Yes, Sir. I think only the very best teachers were employed by Lady Catherine de Bourgh of Rosings for her daughter. From her benevolence, I benefitted in many ways."

Abigail looked up from where she was sitting, her skirts spread out in a fan around her. "Oh, la, I always think it is the very place and duty of people in high estate to help those of the poorer class. I know I try to find little ways to be of assistance and Lucinda always tried to do so, did she not, Robert?"

"Indeed. Miss Collins, please to take some lemonade. It is quite cooling."

"Thank you." Catherine wished fervently that she could sit in the shade of a parasol, but in all the hurry and scurry of changing her clothes, she had forgotten to give one to Bessie to bring with her. She was forced to sit and listen to Abigail being poisonously sweet. At least she had her straw hat to protect her from the sun and was only sad that the red ribbons had blown away in her mad galloping ride. They had belonged to Bennetta and were a reminder of her dark-eyed cousin. She wondered what that young lady would have thought of Abigail and her lips twitched in a secret smile.

"I see you find our demeanour amusing, Miss Collins." Martin smiled at her, leaning up on one elbow and raising a glass to her in a mock toast.

"No, certainly not. I was remembering my ride here, that was all."

"You must be hungry. I am sure Matilda is, too. Let me help you both to some food. Here is cold pigeon pie - a slice for you, Matilda. Miss Collins? No, then some cheese, perhaps, or a jelly that, considering its extremely wobbly state, has not travelled very well!"

Abigail was trying to make Matilda say please before she took a glass of lemonade. "Come, come, Matilda. You are not trying. It is such an easy little word. Please. There, now you say it after me."

Catherine threw a swift glance at her young charge. She could tell by the mutinous set of her lips and the way she hung her head so her hair covered her cheeks and hid her expression, that she was not happy. Oh, Abigail obviously meant well and if she was indeed going to be Matilda's step-mother then she had every right to try and coach her, but this was not the way to do it.

Martin was apparently of the same mind. "Lord, Abigail, leave the child alone. We're having a picnic; this is not the time for lessons. I want to hear all about your visit to London last week. I yearn for gossip; to know who is courting whom, what is the latest fashion for men. I believe waists on coats are now to be very small, which is ideal for slim gentlemen but not for those of a more rotund disposition! I have been away from London for far too long. Miss Collins, I beg for your opinion. Consider my shape - do you think a tight waisted coat will suit me?"

Sir Robert jabbed his knife into the slice of beef before him with undue violence. He felt completely and utterly at a loss to define what he was feeling. Here, next to Abigail, was all the quiet normality that he was used to. She was an old friend; all cool elegance and behaviour. She didn't stir his emotions, uncover unwelcome feelings that he had never experienced before, not even with his wife.

But on the other side of the group sat a small figure wearing a ridiculous straw hat, that, without ribbons, was perched precariously on her head, the daughter of a country parson, a girl who was a good ten years younger than him. She had no elegance but every time he was in her company, she showed him a joy of living and laughter that he knew he had not experienced since he was a very young boy. And Martin was flirting with her!

He didn't blame his brother - he knew that Martin would flirt with any available female. But it was reprehensible of Miss Collins to sit there in her silly hat and smile at his antics with a very loose setting jelly that was trying to escape off his spoon onto the grass.

"Bessie - thank you, we will serve ourselves. Perhaps you should take this opportunity to accompany Miss Matilda to visit your grandmother. I believe the village is just over the crest of the hill. And Miss Collins - I would be grateful if you would go as well."

Catherine sprang to her feet, glad to be away from Abigail's belittling gaze. "Certainly - come Matilda, we shall follow Bessie. Hold my hand tightly and stay by my side."

"I shall come, too." Martin began to get up but his brother waved him down.

"No need to disturb yourself, Martin. I fear we will only worry the old lady if too many people descend on her small home."

"Yes, Martin, leave it to those who are used to visiting homes in such conditions." Abigail tilted her parasol so that no one would see her face.

Martin reclined on the rugs again and lifted his lemonade to his lips, wondering if he could add a little something from his hip flask without Robert seeing. From where he was lying he could see that his brother was apparently paying close attention to what Abigail was saying, but his gaze was following the three small figures as they vanished along the dusty lane.

Once over the crest of the grassy ridge, Catherine could see the brilliant wrinkled blue of the sea stretching away into the far horizon. A breeze cooled her hot face and she undid her heavy jacket.

"Why - I can see the battlements of Courtney Castle over the top of that headland! So close. I thought we were further away."

"We go inland a fair way with the carriage to avoid the bay," Bessie said. "But when tide is out you can walk along the beach to my village. It be quicker than going by road, but gentry don't like to do it because of being splashed by the waves. And the tide does come in something real fast and you would not care to be stranded on the rocks and having to be rescued."

Catherine laughed. "Certainly not! But Matilda and I love walking along the tide line, looking for shells and pieces of jet that are hidden in these cliffs, don't we?"

She smiled down warmly at the child whose hand was clasped so affectionately in her own. Matilda nodded and for a second Catherine was sure she was going to speak, then she turned away once more.

"You can just see Granma's cottage from here, too," Bessie said and pointed towards the rocky coast line. In the distance, Catherine could just make out a dwelling standing outside of the village. She could see a chimney with a wisp of smoke and a roof heavy with moss. Only a thin pathway separated the cottage from the steep pebbled beach that fell away towards the rocks and sea and she could only imagine how dangerous it must be when the winter storms drove the tides higher and higher.

"Is your grandmother not scared to live so close to the sea? What happens during a storm?"

Bessie laughed. "Oh, Granma holds no fear of the sea. If it gets very bad, she climbs upstairs with the cat and her little valuables, but she always reckons that nobody ever died from wet feet."

Suddenly Matilda pulled hard at Catherine's arm and pointed too, but further along the coast where the cliffs rose up in great rocky slabs.

"What is it, Matilda? What do you see?"

"I reckon little lass is showing you the caves me Granma talks about in her stories, Miss."

Catherine laughed. "Oh the ones made of emeralds and pearls! Wouldn't that be lovely if it were true. We could run down and help ourselves. Yes, Matilda, I can see a dark patch or two. Perhaps they are magical caves. Who knows?"

"You don't want to encourage her, Miss Collins," Bessie said roughly. "Those caves can be dangerous places. You wouldn't want to be exploring them. Best left well alone."

A ten minute walk down the rough path brought them to the front of the cottage. The breeze was growing stronger now and Catherine was glad when Bessie pushed open the door and, calling out to her grandmother, ushered them all inside.

There was no hallway, the door opened straight into the main room. It seemed dark after the bright sunlight, the windows were small and only a little light entered, filtered in blue and green by the pieces of sea washed glass that hung on strings from above the windowpanes.

Catherine hadn't been at all sure what to expect. She was interested to see the place where Lucinda Courtney had come with her young daughter. It was hard to reconcile her image of the beautiful, elegant woman whom people spoke about with this fisherman's cottage. Had she sat where Catherine was now sitting, listening to the old woman speaking? Surely, she hadn't partaken of the strong ale or eaten the rough oat bread that would have been offered to a guest?

A strong smell of fish hung in the air, but also the more homely aroma of cooking. Even on this hot day, a fire was burning against the cold of the stone walls and a kettle was singing on its hob. The inside of the cottage had been whitewashed and the floor flagstones freshly scrubbed. A very old lady was sitting in a rocking chair by the fire with a great ginger cat sitting on the patchwork quilt which covered her lap.

To Catherine's delight and astonishment, Matilda gave a little sound and dropping Catherine's hand, ran across the room. She sank onto her knees by the rocking chair and stroked the cat as if it was an old friend.

The old lady looked up from under a bonnet bleached white from many washings. She didn't look well, tired and drawn, but her dark eyes in her wrinkled face were still welcoming.

"Miss Collins, this is my granma, Mrs Stokes. Me da is a fisherman and out with his boat. This is Miss Collins, Gran - Miss Matilda's governess. She likes our stories I tell the little miss at bed time."

"Welcome, welcome, hinnie! Sit down, Miss. Rest yourself. Bessie, pour ale."

Catherine sank down into a chair on the other side of the fireplace. "Thank you, Bessie, but please don't go to any trouble." She was not at all sure of the strength of drink she might be given. It would be impolite to ask for it to be watered down but she could just imagine the look on Sir Robert's face if she returned smelling of strong drink.

The old lady nodded; Matilda's sun bonnet had slipped down and was lying across her back, held by its ribbons. A gnarled hand ran softly down the bright fair hair, and she muttered something in a strong dialect that Catherine couldn't quite understand.

Bessie said, "Granma is delighted to see the little Miss again. Mrs Courtney often brought her to visit but, of course, Maister would have known nought about that."

"I am sure he would have tried to continue the visits if he had known," Catherine replied and hoped she was right. Matilda was smiling widely and had curled herself up on the footstool at the old lady's feet. It had been wonderful to hear the small sound she had made when she noticed the cat. Surely this was a good sign that one day the child would speak again; she was anxious to tell Sir Robert the news. How could she make him see that Matilda would speak when she was ready and that all the forcing in the world would not help.

As if knowing by instinct what the child wanted, Mrs Stokes began to talk. Her voice was soft and the accent was difficult for Catherine to hear and understand, but Matilda seemed to have no problem at all. It was a long, rambling story about a beautiful mermaid who lived in an emerald cave and Catherine thought she heard the mention of three wishes and a handsome prince.

She smiled to herself as the homely crackling of the fire began to relax her and she listened to the sing-song voice weaving its old tale of beauty and evil and wishes that would make everything right in the world.

She was gazing dreamily out of the window, realising that the dark blue glass was exactly the same shade as Sir Robert's eyes and wondering why she should have noticed that fact when footsteps sounded loudly on the pebbles outside and with a tap at the door, it swung open and the man himself stood there.

"Good afternoon, Mrs Stokes." Sir Robert swept off his hat and bending slightly to avoid the low lintel, entered the cottage. "Pray do not disturb yourself," he hastened to add as the old lady began to struggle to her feet. "Miss Collins, Matilda, we have taken up enough of the good lady's time. We have packed up the picnic and are ready to set out for home. Make your curtsey, Matilda. I know she would say thank you if she could, Mrs Stokes. Miss Collins, I shall lead the mare back. I will not need to examine your riding skills again."

"Thank you, Sir. Come, Matilda. Thank you, Mrs Stokes for the lovely story."

There was a swirl of movement and Catherine thought she caught the glimpse of silver passing from Sir Robert to the old lady who cackled in appreciation, showing bare gums. "Don't forget to wish, hinnie," she called after them as they left and Catherine wondered which of them she was speaking to.

Outside, Catherine was astounded to find that the sun had slid down the sky and was now only just visible over the crest of the hills. They must have been listening to the stories for a much longer time than she had realised. Matilda was now very tired and stumbled on the pebbles as they climbed out of the village.

Without speaking, Sir Robert picked her up and carried her the rest of the way. Catherine hurried to keep up with his long stride, well aware that Bessie was having no trouble coping with the steep slope. She was almost glad he did not speak as she didn't think she had the breath to reply to him.

But eventually they reached the crest of the hill and could see the carriage and pony trap waiting for them. Martin was holding the reins of the two horses and handed them over to his brother when he had helped Bessie into the trap and tenderly deposited Matilda next to her.

Sir Robert turned to Catherine. "Will you travel in the carriage or in the trap, Miss Collins?"

Catherine flushed. Was he asking her to choose her place in the castle's hierarchy? Did he see her as a servant or as a guest? Once again she had the feeling that he was playing with her emotions. If he disliked her and wanted her gone from Courtney, he only had to say: there was no need for this charade.

She turned towards the pony trap but just as she was about to pull herself up to sit next to Matilda, she felt a pair of hands on her waist and Martin was spinning her round and pushing her gently towards the carriage.

"Oh, do sit with us, dear Miss Collins. Abigail is almost asleep, and I fear that if you do not talk sensibly to me of sensible things, I will be, too. There!" He half lifted her into the carriage to sit opposite Miss Richmond and then swung himself in afterwards.

For a moment she thought he was going to take the place next to her, but instead he chose to lounge opposite, his eyes gleaming with mischief. The groom urged the horses forward and the carriage and trap made their way in stately fashion towards the castle. A few minutes later, Sir Robert galloped past, leading the mare on a short rein and was soon out of sight.

The journey home was undertaken almost in silence. Martin's flirtatious comments to Catherine were greeted with studious silence on her behalf and Abigail said nothing at all. Catherine would almost have believed she was asleep, except that the hand holding the parasol was white at the knuckles and the shade shook slightly as if in a strong wind.

She was more than happy when they arrived back at the castle and she and Bessie could hurry Matilda indoors. There was no sign of Sir Robert in the stable yard, but Catherine could see one of the grooms walking his horses to cool them down. From the sweat on their necks, they had been ridden hard.

Matilda was almost asleep on her feet and Catherine decided that it would be best if she had some bread and warm sweet milk in her room before going straight to bed. She left Bessie to her night time ministrations, knowing that the girl cherished these quiet moments alone with the child. As much as Catherine would have enjoyed brushing Matilda's hair and tying the ribbons on her nightgown, she knew that she would forfeit Bessie's cooperation if she did.

Safely in her room, Catherine threw herself across her bed, aching all over from too much walking and too much sun. Her head ached and she would have willingly washed and gone straight to sleep if she had had a choice. But she knew she had to change and present herself downstairs for dinner.

She gave herself an hour, trying to relax and then forced herself up to find the coolest dress she could to wear, a pale green gauze that had again once belonged to Bennetta. There would be no need of a shawl tonight.

The summer evenings were long these days, darkness didn't fall until very late in the evening. The mullioned windows of the breakfast room, that was now being used for small family dinners, were wide open to let in the soft, warm air. The heat of the day was lingering late into the evening with the promise of another very hot day to come. Catherine could hear the distant cries of the ever-present gulls that circled around over the incoming tide, hunting for their own supper.

Lady Honoria was being served her meal upstairs that evening and so the four of them sat in an uneasy atmosphere at the table. Sir Robert was polite but distant, asking Catherine only that he hoped Matilda had not over tired herself. Abigail had obviously recovered her spirits and was all wit and elegance, presiding over the table as if she were already Lady Courtney and Martin kept the conversation going with a light-hearted remark every time it faltered and stopped.

At last, the fruit course was cleared away and they moved from the dining-table into the drawing-room for coffee and hot chocolate.

Abigail spread the skirts of her dark gold velvet dress over the sofa and shut her fan with a little snap. "Well, I think we can say our picnic was a great success, Robert, do you not agree? You discovered that Miss Collins will not fall off a horse at the first opportunity and we three spent a delightful hour or two remembering all the happy times we've spent together and planning for the dinner party. And as much as we all adore Matilda, I think we can agree that it is always pleasant to have a short time without children and servants in close attendance."

Catherine fought down the temptation to make a cold reply to that remark but Sir Robert was busy at the writing desk, his quill scratching across the paper as he wrote and she thought it best to pretend she hadn't heard. After all, it was not her place to do so.

'And why should that bother you?' she asked herself. 'Why should you care so much what he thinks about you?' She tried to tell herself that of course it was important, that he was her employer and as such she needed him to have a good opinion of her. There was nothing else and she banished from her mind the minutes she had spent in the little fisherman's cottage, deciding which piece of blue glass matched the colour of Sir Robert's eyes!

Martin finished his coffee and sprang to his feet. "Let us have some music! Abigail, will you play for us?"

"Oh, I am far too tired this evening, Martin. I spent a good hour in my room before dinner, writing out the invitations to the party and sending them off for immediate delivery. My fingers are quite fatigued. Surely Miss Collins will be able to delight us with a few homely tunes."

"Yes, come Catherine. Nothing too elaborate or clever. Just some good old-fashioned melodies - that is what I find I desire tonight. Let us look through all this music here. I'm sure we can find something that will delight us."

Catherine felt it would be discourteous to refuse. If the tune was simple enough, she knew she could manage not to look too foolish. She joined Martin at the pianoforte and together they started sorting the sheet music. Abigail got up and crossed the room to where her host was just finishing his letter.

"Do stop and rest for a while, Robert. I am sure it is not good for you to still be working."

He looked up with a smile. "All done. Just a legal letter I needed to send." He glanced across the room. "Are we to have music?"

Abigail sank into a chair beside him and fanned herself vigorously. "I declare it is getting hotter this evening; I think we are in for a heatwave. Yes, indeed we are to have music. I thought it only fair that Miss Collins has a chance to show off her talents to Martin, however poor they may prove. Don't you think they make a handsome couple, although I feel she will be sadly upset if she sets her cap at him!"

Sir Robert glanced across at the couple by the pianoforte - Catherine was sitting, looking up at Martin and laughing at some remark he had just made. "Martin always makes himself agreeable to young women. He flirts with you at every opportunity."

"Oh Robert, you know he means nothing by that! It is just a silly habit he formed when we were all very young. But perhaps he is truly growing fond of Miss Collins. Would that be such a dreadful match? She has no wealth to bring him, that is true, but she is a steady sort of girl and that might be just the sort of wife he needs."

"Martin is in no position to marry anyone," Sir Robert said, his voice terse as he banged his seal down hard on the back of his envelope where the soft wax was waiting. "And I have seen no signs of any growing attachment between the two of them. He has hardly known her more than a few days."

Abigail lowered her eyes modestly. "But when you fall in love Robert, it takes no more than a second."

There was a long pause. Surely, she thought, this was the moment when he would declare himself? She had as good as told him what her feelings were. What was he waiting for? But there was no response apart from a frowning glance at the girl at the piano and his brother, laughing as he made a muddle in turning the pages of the music.

"So Robert, come and sit by me and let me tell you all the plans I have been making with Mrs Crawford for the dinner party before the ball. Oh, don't look so aghast, my dear! It is not to be a grand affair, just close friends of ours and some neighbours whom we must honour with an invite for dinner as well dancing. Cook is apparently delighted that she can try her hand at some more elaborate dishes."

Sir Robert nodded, trying hard to accept that this was how his future life would be if he proposed to Abigail. She would make a wonderful hostess and when she got used to Matilda, a good mother. There was nothing, nothing to stop him proposing to her right now and they could announce it on the evening of the dinner party. So why did he feel as if the floor was not firm beneath his feet and why did he have the overwhelming urge to walk across the room and take Martin's place at the pianoforte? He stood, fingering in his pocket a length of red ribbon that he had forgotten to return to its owner.

The tune came to an end and Catherine stood up, shaking her head at Martin who was insisting on another piece. She walked across to the open window and sat on the window seat, gazing out into where the summer sky was finally darkening and stars were beginning to appear.

Martin turned his attention to Abigail who eventually gave in with a little laugh to his demands and sitting at the piano began to play with exquisite tone and touch. After listening for a few minutes, Sir Robert joined Catherine at the window.

"I trust you are not too fatigued from your riding today, Miss Collins?"

She shook her head. "Not at all. I may ache a little tomorrow but it will soon vanish. May I ask, have you finally decided that Matilda shall have a pony?"

He was silent for a while, watching as a footman entered the room and began to light the many candles. Then, "Yes, I must learn not to be so stupidly fearful for her wellbeing. You have shown me that she will be as safe as possible in your care and with her affliction I am loathe to deny her anything that gives her pleasure. As you are aware, it is her seventh birthday soon - the day after the dinner party. The pony will be a good present for her."

Catherine smiled up at him. He had earlier shed his jacket and she could feel the warmth of his arm against her own, only the thin layer of linen separating them. "She will be so pleased."

They fell silent again but it was a comfortable silence, neither apparently needing to speak but happy to watch the bats begin to flit in the darkness as they began their night-time hunt. Sir Robert felt a flood of emotion tear through him; this was happiness, this was delight, this must be -

A discordant note sounded loudly from the piano and the moment was broken as Abigail and Martin both broke into laughter at her mistake. Sir Robert took a deep breath. "Are you happy here, Miss Collins?"

Catherine wished he wouldn't sit so close to her. She had no right to feel as if he was the only person in the world who mattered to her. And now he was asking if she were happy? What should be her reply. "Yes, when I am with you. Yes, when I look at you or hear your voice. That I am lonely when you are not there."

She glanced across the room to where the dark haired, elegant woman sitting at the piano had made some teasing remark to Martin. There was the future Lady Courtney. Soon she and Sir Robert would surely be engaged and Catherine could return to Hertfordshire and her duties to her step-mother and half-sister.

Sir Robert followed her gaze and saw, for an instant, a bleak sorrow cross her face. So, she did care for Martin and was upset to see him flirting so vigorously with Abigail. He could feel her arm trembling against his and fought to control his feelings. He knew for a certainty that Martin would never marry Catherine Collins. Martin would marry an heiress or nobody. His brother was far too fond of his easy lifestyle to settle down to family life on the allowance the Courtney estate made him every month and it broke his heart to see this bright-spirited girl so downcast.

"Very happy. I love Matilda and I have great hopes of her progress. Sometimes I am certain that she is on the verge of speaking and surely one day with gentle encouragement she will do so."

"I pray that is so. I am grateful for all your care. I fear I have not made this clear before."

'But I don't want your gratitude,' Catherine thought bitterly, even as she bowed her head in acknowledgement of his compliment. 'That is not what I want at all.'

Sir Robert sent another piercing glance across the room to where the flickering candles illuminated Martin and Abigail at the piano. "My brother - " he began - "I feel I should warn you - " He stopped, realising that he was venturing too far down a very indelicate road.

Catherine felt the hot colour flood up into her cheeks. Did this aggravating man really think she was interested in Martin? Did he believe she had such a light-weight character that he would appeal to her as a husband? What was worse, did he imagine she had been setting her cap at him? Oh, it was all too unbearable!

Before she could reply or even move, there was the sound of laughter outside the door and a footman entered, obviously trying not to smile. "Sir Robert, a lady to see you and Miss Collins."

"Who – what?"

Catherine stood up, puzzled. She knew no one in Northumberland who would call to see her, especially not at this time of the evening when it was almost dark outside.

With a rush of cherry red cloak, her bonnet slipping off her long dark curls, a girl burst into the room, her dark eyes sparkling. It was Miss Bennetta Darcy.

9

"Bennetta!"

"Why, it's young Miss Darcy!" Martin sounded delighted.

Bennetta smiled round the room and then turned her attention to her host. "Sir Robert!" She dropped a graceful curtsey. "I must apologise most humbly for my unexpected arrival and so late in the evening, too."

Sir Robert took her outstretched hand and bowed over it. "Miss Bennetta! I welcome you to Courtney Castle, although I admit your arrival has both astonished and alarmed me. Are you travelling on your own? What brings you north in this fashion?"

"Robert - allow her to sit and regain her breath and please be so kind as to introduce us."

"Of course, I am remiss. Miss Bennetta Darcy - Miss Abigail Richmond, a great friend of our family and you have, of course, met my brother at Richard's wedding."

Two brief curtsies and a bow from Martin, then Bennetta turned and took Catherine's hand. "It is so good to see you Cousin Catherine."

Catherine was bewildered. "But Bennetta, whatever are you doing here? It is lovely to see you but..."

"La - please don't be alarmed! I apologise again. Sir Robert, I have left my maid in the care of your housekeeper and my coachman is, I am sure, being well looked after by your servants. I know the hour is late, but we were supposed to arrive this afternoon. Sadly, one of the horses threw a shoe and we had to find a smithy and then something else broke and had to be repaired and so were delayed."

She smiled round the room. "I am on my way to Scotland, to stay with my Aunt Georgiana for a few weeks. My parents thought it a good idea to call in to see our cousin Catherine. I have letters for her and parcels. And here, too, Sir Robert, I have letters from your brother and sister in Derbyshire. I fear they are rather short as I called in to see them on my way north and they were written in a hurry. Mama made it clear that I should not impose on you for more than an hour or so, but now I fear I must ask for a bed as well!"

Sir Robert smiled down at the vivacious young woman as she handed over the letters and Catherine remarked to herself, once again, how different his stern features looked when he smiled.

"We will be delighted for you to stay. But surely not just for one night. Can you not make a little visit here at Courtney? Messages can be sent to your aunt in Scotland. I am sure Miss Collins will be delighted to have time to hear all your news from Pemberley and her own family, of course."

"And we are to hold a dance in a few days' time." Martin smiled at Bennetta and she lowered her eyes demurely so that he should not see the acceptance of the boldness of his gaze. "Surely you can stay for that?"

"La, I would have enjoyed that more than anything. But sadly, I think Papa would not be pleased if I broke my journey for too long. I can stay for one day and then I must leave. And now, Catherine, if you could show me to my room? The housekeeper kindly said she would prepare one immediately." She stood up, tossing back the long dark curls that fell to her shoulders, escaping their pins. "Sir Robert - Mr Martin - Miss Richmond - I bid you goodnight."

Catherine hurried to her side; the young girl did indeed look very tired and pale now; obviously her long journey was proving costly. With Mrs Crawford bustling in front of them, the two girls climbed the spiral staircase in silence, Bennetta leaning heavily on Catherine's arm.

At last, they reached one of the guest rooms where a maid wearing the Pemberley dark blue with a white apron was already unpacking a small travel bag. Mrs Crawford fussed around for a few more moments, checking that there was hot water in the ewer and insisting that a warm brick would be brought up for the bed, even though it was still a hot summer night outside the cool castle walls.

But at last she left and dismissing her maid until the morning, Bennetta threw herself onto the bed and kicked off her shoes, all signs of weariness suddenly vanishing. Catherine smiled to herself; she had forgotten what a good actress the youngest Darcy girl could be when she chose.

"Oh, it is good to see you again, Catherine, and I am delighted that you are wearing one of my dresses. That pale green suits you so well. I cannot believe how hot it is for Northumberland. I do declare it grew hotter as we travelled north, rather than colder. See, here are letters for you and in that large bag over there are some more things that Mama thought you might need. What fun to be here in a castle. It is worth being sent from home in disgrace."

"In disgrace? Oh Bennetta, what have you done?"

"Oh foo! Papa made such a fuss about nothing. Really, he is impossible; he is getting stricter and stricter as he grows older. How he expects his daughters to marry when he prevents us from getting to know young gentlemen, I cannot imagine. He and Anne have already had angry words. She believes he is blighting her chances of matrimony, although who would want to marry a proud, arrogant girl like her I cannot imagine."

Catherine tried to stop the smile that was threatening to cross her face. "Which young gentleman did Mr Darcy take exception to this time?"

Bennetta shrugged then grinned mischievously. "His name is Benjamin and he's an actor. He has the most wonderful dark brown eyes. When he looks at you, you seem to melt."

Catherine closed her eyes for a second, trying not to imagine Mr Darcy's reaction to his daughter's latest conquest. "An actor?"

"A very good one! He is appearing at Drury Lane Theatre in a small part. It was my birthday treat and I chose to go and see *The Merchant of Venice*. I am seventeen now, you know. Quite grown up."

"But how did you meet him?"

"There was a small soirée after the performance and I sent round a note, asking him to attend."

"Bennetta! What were you thinking of? No girl of good family acts in such a way."

Her cousin bounced off the bed and began to pull items out of her baggage. "That's what Mama and Papa said when they heard. They weren't in London with me and the twins - they were at home because Aunt Jane is still very poorly after having little Alethea. But, of course, tattaltale Miss Smith, who was chaperoning us, wrote and told them. They made such a fuss and insisted I return to Pemberley immediately and then said I must go and stay with Aunt Georgiana for the rest of the summer.

"At first, I was upset because nothing exciting ever happens up in Scotland, unless you enjoy fishing, then I realised I could break the journey here in Northumberland and see you. I want to hear all the gossip. I see Mr Martin Courtney is living here, too. Is he a beau of yours? We danced together at Cassandra's wedding - twice - and he brought me an ice. He is certainly very elegant, is he not? And who is that other lady?"

Catherine broke in to the stream of chatter. "Mr Martin is certainly not my beau! He is a gentleman who believes all women should bow down and worship him. He does no work and borrows money from his brother which Sir Robert can ill afford. Miss Abigail Richmond is a friend of the Courtney family: they have known each other since childhood. I have not had any long conversations with her, so as to her character, I can only guess. But it is rumoured she is to be the next Lady Courtney."

She turned away as she spoke, not wanting Bennetta to see the pain that thought caused, unaware that the younger girl could see her quite plainly in the dressing-table mirror.

"Indeed! Well, Sir Robert seems a pleasant man, but stern. He certainly made me welcome, but he does not smile as much as his brother or have the caring expression of their other brother, dear Cassandra's husband."

"He may not have a ready smile, but he cares passionately about his daughter and the Courtney estate," cried Catherine and then fell silent, wondering if she had said too much.

"Oh, I am sure he does. I sometimes wonder if the quietest of men have the deepest feelings. I mean, look at my own dear papa."

Catherine nodded in agreement; she believed this implicitly but talking about Sir Robert's feelings was too difficult for her and she changed the subject, listening eagerly as Bennetta related all that had befallen the Darcy family since they last met.

"As I told you earlier, Aunt Jane is not at all well. Mama is very concerned about her. But the baby thrives."

"And the twins?"

Bennetta tossed her head. "As I said earlier, Anne is as opinionated as ever. She argues with Papa all the time. Jane tries to keep the peace, but Anne just ignores her. Oh, and we are to have our portraits painted around Christmas time by the famous Edmund Avery but whether that will be all five of us children or just the girls, I'm not sure. Fitzwilliam and Henry are horrified at the thought - Fitz because it will take time away from his precious books and studies and Henry because he finds it impossible to stay still for two minutes altogether, let alone pose for a portrait!"

An hour of happy gossip passed and finally Catherine said goodnight and went to her own room. Wearily she undressed, brushed her hair and pulling a robe over her nightgown and with a candle flickering in its holder, tiptoed through the day nursery into the night nursery. Then she stopped, a little gasp escaping her. Sir Robert was standing by the side of the bed, gazing down at his sleeping daughter. Matilda was fast asleep, her long fair hair lying in a fan across the lace of her pillow.

He turned and smiled, putting his finger to his lips. Silently he crossed the room to her side and escorted her back into the day nursery. "I have sent Bessie for fresh water for the bedside. It is such a hot night, Matilda may well wake and be thirsty."

"Do you wish me to wait with her until Bessie returns?"

Sir Robert gazed at her face, the light from the candle flickering across it in gold flashes. "No, that is kind of you, but you must be very tired. I will wait."

There was a silence; Catherine knew she should leave him, he was standing too close, she could feel the heat from his body, knew he was trembling, as was she.

"Catherine - " He spoke as if the word was forced from him against his will. She glanced up, but couldn't see his face clearly in the dark. She raised the candle and just then the passage door to the night nursery opened and she could see that Bessie was back, carrying a jug of water.

"I will see you tomorrow, Miss Collins," Sir Robert said abruptly and walked back to the child's bed without another word.

In a whirl of emotions, Catherine returned to her own room. What had Sir Robert been about to say to her. Oh, why had Bessie come back at that very moment? She sat on her bed, trying to calm her thoughts. Her letters from home were there and she took them up eagerly, glad of any distraction.

Her Cousin Elizabeth's was brief but warm in tone, the writing firm on the expensive linen thread paper. She hoped Catherine was well and that her duties were not too arduous. She explained that she was sending a parcel of garments that had been purchased but never worn by any of her daughters and hoped they would come in useful up in the colder north. The last paragraph was enlightening;

"....Bennetta's last escapade was really upsetting to Mr Darcy and myself. Striking up a liaison with a young actor. If he had been an amiable young man with a good character, we might have ignored the whole thing, knowing that, like all of her fancies, this would not have lasted more than a month or so. But Mr Darcy discovered he was a dissolute roue with a bad reputation. Apparently, this was common knowledge to everyone except Bennetta. He turned her head and she began to say she would like to go on the stage herself!! I need not tell you how my husband reacted to that! And so we are sending her north to Georgiana. A summer spent in the heather and mountains should cool her head and calm her restless spirit."

"Oh goodness - I'm glad I wasn't there when Bennetta told her father she wanted to become an actress. I'm surprised the walls of Pemberley are still standing."

With a smile Catherine turned to her other missives. The one from her stepmother was all blots and crossings-out and full of little Harriet's everyday life, the clever things she said and did and how, Turner, the nursery-maid sent from Pemberley was far superior in every way to Catherine. Then she reached the last paragraph and it sent a chill running through her.

"....indeed, Catherine, I am loathe to send Turner back to Pemberley when your time in Northumberland is over. We have changed your bedroom into a day nursery for Harriet and Turner has her old room for herself. It is difficult to see how we could make changes again in a few months' time. Perhaps Sir

Robert could recommend you to others of his acquaintance who might be in need of a governess."

Sinking down onto her bed, Catherine stared around her, feeling scared and very alone. She had given no serious thought as to what would happen when Sir Robert married and Matilda had a step-mother. She had vaguely imagined that she would return to Longbourn and take up her role as elder sister to Harriet. Lately she had pushed all those thoughts away because they meant she had to imagine Sir Robert marrying Abigail and, for some reason, she couldn't bear to think of that.

Now, however, she realised she might well be homeless when the marriage took place. She couldn't see Abigail allowing her to remain as Matilda's governess, no, she wouldn't want anyone to influence Sir Robert in a way opposed to her own. For all her kind words, caresses and smiles, Catherine had the strongest suspicion Miss Richmond did not like Matilda and that the little girl would be sent off to live in seclusion somewhere a long way away. And there was no way she, herself, would want to stay here once Abigail became Lady Courtney.

Then her common-sense came to the fore. Of course, she would not be homeless - if all failed, she knew Cousin Elizabeth would let her stay at Pemberley until she could find another position. And the other thing she knew was that she could never ask Sir Robert for help. To have him know that she was held in such low regard by her own family was unbearable. To imagine him feeling sorry for her was more than she could possibly endure, and she resolutely put from her mind the sound of his voice saying her name in the warm dark of the day nursery.

Bennetta rose very early the next morning to the sound of screeching gulls and waves breaking on the rocks below her window. The sun was already warm on her face when she opened her window and it was clearly going to be another very hot day. She was glad that she could at least spend this one outdoors and not shut up in the carriage, travelling along the lonely dusty roads towards Scotland.

When her maid had helped her dress in the lightest of pale blue muslins, she remembered that there was one person she had yet to see before she left the castle. A housemaid, busy sweeping the long corridor outside her room, directed her to the other side of the castle and when she tapped on a door, an elderly maid opened it, gazing at her with suspicion.

"Miss Bennetta Darcy to see Lady Honoria, if you please. My apologies for calling at such an early hour."

"Stop lurking in the doorway, child, and come in!" The voice was old and thin but still full of vigour.

Bennetta made her way into the room where Sir Robert's elderly aunt was sitting, gazing out of the window to the sea many feet below. The room was quite dark; the windows were smaller this high up in the castle and what sunlight did enter had to do battle against the dark tapestries and rugs that covered the walls and floor.

Dressed all in purple with a fine rug over her lap, she glanced up to look at her visitor. "Miss Bennetta Darcy! I heard that you had arrived at Courtney. I'm glad to see that your parents have installed some modicum of manners in you. That you realised it would be most remiss to leave before tendering your attentions to myself."

Bennetta curtsied. She had met Lady Honoria at Cassandra's wedding: she had admired the huge hat she had worn and the fact that she didn't seem to care an iota as to what the rest of the world thought of her. She had learnt of the old lady's past from Richard Courtney and envied the exciting life she had led.

"I bring respectful greetings from my mama and papa, Lady Honoria, and from Richard and Cassandra, of course."

"Hmmp. Hard to imagine those two love-birds would have thoughts of anyone but themselves yet. Yes, yes, well, sit, sit, child. Stop lurking over the top of me like some squawking parrot. I will write to your mother, thanking her. I like Elizabeth Darcy. The most sensible thing your father ever did was to marry her.

"Ha! And what a commotion that caused, Miss Eliza Bennet, a person of no importance, catching the attention of one of England's wealthiest bachelors! I still have the letters written to me by Fitzwilliam's aunt! Lord, she was not impressed by the match. There are tears in the paper where her pen was being used so forcefully."

Bennetta kept silent. She had not realised that Lady Honoria had known her Great Aunt Catherine. The world, it seemed, was a very small place. It was, however, disconcerting to think that she had known papa before he married mama.

"So - they've sent you away from all the temptations of London and Pemberley, have they? Some young man, I suppose - no, no - I don't want to hear the details!" She held up a wrinkled hand, the great ruby ring glowing on her finger as the sunlight touched it. "I like a gal who has the courage to break out of the constraints of duty and family, as long as you keep your head and don't lose your heart."

Bennetta smiled. "I was never in danger of doing that, but Papa refused to believe me. So I am banished to the hills and lochs, to spend time with my cousin Flora at Tawny Castle where they insist on putting salt on their morning porridge instead of honey."

"Ha! A great hardship indeed! I take it there are no temptations for young ladies amongst the heather?"

Bennetta sighed. "Not that I have ever seen, but I live in hopes. But at least my banishment has given me an opportunity to see Catherine and report back to Mama. I know she has been worried about her, concerned that she did the right thing in recommending her to Sir Robert."

"And how did you find your cousin?"

Bennetta hesitated. "I do not know her well. We hardly met before Cassandra's wedding. I would have said she was a very level-headed girl, not one to suffer from emotional highs or lows. Indeed, my family always remark on her common-sense if her name is mentioned."

"And now?"

"Oh she seems happy enough, but I get the feeling that she is deeply sad about something. Of course, that may well just be my imagination. Mama says I have far too much of that for my own good."

"Perhaps Catherine worries about Matilda?"

"I am sure you are right. The child's affliction must concern her greatly."

"Or perhaps that scoundrel, Martin, has been flirting with her? He has the ability to turn any gal's head if he puts his mind to it."

"No - Catherine is far too sensible to be swayed by a handsome face and pretty words."

"Well, well, we shall just have to wait and see. I have my own ideas of what her arrival here has achieved. Time will tell if I am right. But are you likely to be swayed in that direction, Miss? Will you fall for a handsome face and sweet words?"

Bennetta looked suddenly serious. "It is 1833 and I am seventeen years of age but have no role in life. I've always felt third choice amongst the Darcy girls. I have no place in the family - oh, I know my mama loves me dearly, Lady Honoria, but my papa...? Sometimes he looks at me with such displeasure, as if I have offended him personally.

"He told me once that I am too like my Aunt Lydia. I know she is a silly sort of woman in some ways, but I admire her because she has always got what she wanted from life, no matter what the cost. Is that such a bad thing? I feel that there must be something more for me than just being a wife and then a mother. Then I look at Cassandra and Richard together and wonder if I will ever feel like that about another person. I find it hard to believe that I will."

Lady Honoria shut her eyes briefly. She was angry with Fitzwilliam Darcy; his pride had almost cost him the love of the woman who had eventually changed his life. That same pride seemed to have raised its head again where this daughter was concerned. He was so determined that she would not turn out like his flibbertigibbet sister-in-law that he could not see the worth of the young girl in front of him.

She had been such a young girl once; the only daughter of a man who thought women were of no importance. She had married, impulsively, stupidly perhaps, but for love. She'd thought she could change her husband's attitude to the poor people who lived on his estate and maybe she would have succeeded. But she hadn't had time. Her married life in France had ended in blood and disaster but she never regretted a moment of her months with Pierre. For all his many faults, he had loved her dearly, passionately and it was those memories that now kept her old bones warm at night.

When she opened her eyes, Bennetta was staring into the distance, a mutinous expression on her pretty face. The old lady sighed. She had enough worries at the moment dealing with her thick-headed nephew who wouldn't see what was right in front of him and a slip of a girl who had no idea of her own worth. Taking on the troubles of Miss Bennetta Darcy would have to wait for another day. But...

"If you ever have time on your hands, write to me of what you have been doing," she said suddenly. "And call in to see me the next time you pass through Northumberland."

She held out her hand in farewell and Bennetta took it, suddenly serious. "I will write," she said and knew that she would.

When Catherine and Matilda reached the breakfast room it was to find Bennetta finishing her meal. She chatted away to Matilda, ignoring the fact that there was no reply but making the little girl smile as she recounted some of her more alarming escapades when she was growing up.

"Are we late this morning?" Catherine inquired as Mrs Crawford came into the room with more hot rolls. "I have seen no one else."

"Well, Sir Robert was up and away on estate business and took no breakfast at all. Miss Richmond ate in her room and has now gone to Newcastle until tomorrow and Mr Martin has yet to put in an appearance."

"I like Mr. Martin Courtney," Bennetta said, when the housekeeper had left the room. "He makes me laugh. I told you we danced together at Cassandra's wedding, didn't I? Papa was not pleased. I mean it was two dances and sharing one crushed ice! We were hardly likely to elope after that."

Catherine sighed: as much as she was delighted to see her cousin, she was relieved that she would be leaving Courtney the following day. She had noticed the way Martin had looked at her and didn't trust Bennetta not to flirt with him.

"You must write and tell me all about the ball," Bennetta said. "Who comes, who dances with whom, describe all the dresses and how the gentlemen look. Everything to help me cope with my lonely isolation! I like Cousin Flora, but she has no interest in such things." She hesitated. "If Miss Richmond does become Lady Courtney, will you go home?"

Catherine nodded: she couldn't find the words to explain that it looked unlikely she would be going back to Longbourn to live, that where she found a home was in the laps of the gods.

"Eat up, Matilda," she said now. "We will show Miss Darcy all around the castle and the gardens. She will see how much work we have yet to do to make the flower-beds pretty again, but there are blooms to admire and lots of rambling roses. Then perhaps we can walk on the beach to find her some shells. If you have finished, run upstairs and ask Bessie for your stout shoes and a sun bonnet."

"How does she ask?" Bennetta looked surprised as the child ran out of the room.

"Oh, she will point and her maid knows what she will need. Every day I think she is a little closer to speaking, but just when I am sure she will, she seems to stop herself. It is most frustrating."

"You are fond of her?"

Catherine smiled and gathered up her own sunbonnet. "Yes indeed. She is nearly seven, such an enchanting age. I shall miss her dreadfully when it is time for me to leave Courtney."

"But surely there would be a place here for you, even if Sir Robert remarries? I only caught a quick glimpse of her last night, but I do not feel Miss Richmond would be the sort of woman who would get involved in a small girl's day to day life. Especially not one with an affliction."

Catherine turned away so that her face was hidden. "I would not wish to stay here once Sir Robert marries," she said and the tone of her voice forbade Bennetta from enquiring any further.

10

Later that afternoon, Catherine, Bennetta and Matilda were sitting under the shade of their parasols on the rough grassy headland that stretched out into the ocean from the shelter of the castle walls, the sea stretching out smooth and blue to the horizon. They had gathered shells along the tideline in the morning and now Matilda was happily sorting them into piles and patterns.

Martin lounged on the grass at their side, his cravat discarded and the top buttons of his shirt undone against the heat, sipping lemonade a footman had brought down from the castle. He yawned discreetly, getting an immediate response from Bennetta.

"I do declare you are still half asleep, Sir! Shame on you. It is nearly four o'clock."

Martin grinned at her, his eyes bright with mischief. "Fair Bennetta, I only woke when I did because I was dreaming of you and Miss Collins and needed to make certain that you were both as lovely in real life as you were in my dream!"

Bennetta giggled and glanced sideways at him under lowered eyelashes. "Fie, Sir, you are too forward. Poor Catherine's face is going quite pink."

Martin laughed and continued to make a daisy chain from the flowers studding the grass where they sat. "I fear Miss Collins would never be influenced by anything I said. She is a fairy girl and as such has no time for mere mortals."

"A fairy girl?"

"Pay him no attention. Mr Martin is making fun of the fact that when we first met at Pemberley, I was barefoot in the garden."

"And dancing."

"Catherine!" Bennetta threw her cousin a startled look. That certainly did not sound like the girl who was noted in the family for her common-sense.

"You, on the other hand, Miss Bennetta, I believe to be a witch, because you have certainly bewitched me."

There was a long pause and Catherine looked up, suddenly startled. There had been a ring of truth in Martin's voice. Surely he was not developing real feelings for the youngest Darcy girl? If so, he would be grievously disappointed. He was certainly not the type of man that Mr and Mrs Darcy would consider suitable for their daughter.

"There!" Martin had finished the daisy chain and he bestowed it on Catherine's sun bonnet. "I have crowned you queen of the day."

Matilda put her hands over her mouth and her eyes shone as if it was a great joke. Catherine was sure she was going to laugh as Martin turned to her in mock alarm. "Oh you think it funny, do you, Miss? Well, I suggest that we go for a quick paddle along the sandy part of the shore while the tide is out. That will cool you down. What say you, Miss Collins?"

Catherine shook her head. “Take Matilda by all means, Sir. It will do her good to run around a little before supper and I think the heat is subsiding somewhat.”

She watched as, hand in hand, uncle and niece walked down the steps into the sandy bay. They had just reached the water’s edge when Bennetta jumped up.

“I think I will join them. I long to paddle in the sea. Papa is always promising that we shall go bathing one day, but we never do. The boys are allowed to swim in the lake, but we girls just have to sit and watch, although I have taken off my shoes and stockings and paddled on the edge. Papa was furious! ” And before any reply could be made, she was running down the steps to join the couple on the shore.

Catherine stood on the edge of the cliff, watching the three figures on the sand below. She realised that Bennetta and Martin were similar in nature. They were both supremely confident and determined to do exactly what they wanted in life. She felt tears sting her eyes - she could see no future where she could follow her own heart and live the life she wanted.

Sir Robert Courtney had arrived home early, hot and weary. The Courtney estate had been left very rundown during his father’s long illness. At every turn there were people wanting his help, advice, money and most of all, time. He had spent all morning arguing with a builder who was repairing some farm workers’ cottages and using very poor materials.

It was still hot, with a sullen haze on the sea that told him a storm was brewing in the next few days. As he crossed the south hall, he stripped off his coat and pulled off his cravat, handing them to a footman. He was tempted to make his way along the coast to one of the tiny private coves he knew, strip off and swim until his blood cooled.

Mrs Crawford appeared and told him that his daughter, his brother, Miss Darcy and Miss Collins were all out on the headland, enjoying the sunshine. And that his aunt would like a word with him, if he would be so good as to spare her a moment or two.

Lady Honoria's room was shaded from the sunlight and the thick stone castle walls kept it cool. Sir Robert bent his head and kissed her cheek. "You look well, Aunt."

"Which is more than I can say for you! Hot and bothered. Hot and bothered. Not so easy running the estate as you thought, eh?"

"I never thought it would be easy. But my father's loss of interest means so much needs to be done. I sometimes wonder if I will ever catch up. It would be good to have some help, but Martin shows not the slightest interest and Richard has his own career to think about."

Lady Honoria hobbled across the room to the deep window seat, waving away his offer of help. "I am not completely crippled yet! Leave me be." She pulled back the curtain and gazed down to where the headland stretched out from the walls beneath her.

In the far distance she could see the four small figures sitting on the grass, the pretty colours of the parasols. She glanced back at her nephew - tall, dark haired with eyes that used to be full of the joy of living and a mouth that when he smiled had turned his stern demeanour into something far more attractive. She realised it was a long time since she had seen that smile.

"So, there is to be a grand dinner party and dance?"

"Yes, Abigail and Martin seem to think it is right for me to hold one." Sir Robert frowned and pulled at the button on his shirt cuff that was coming loose.

"Don't fidget, boy. It's irritating. Abigail Richmond wants to act as hostess does she?"

"It can do no harm. Abigail thinks I should bring Matilda downstairs, that perhaps new people talking to her will make her speak. The day after the dance it will be her seventh birthday. She must speak soon or perhaps she never will."

"And what does Miss Collins think?"

"Catherine? I mean, Miss Collins." Sir Robert slipped his hand into his pocket without thinking and touched the crimson ribbon that lay hidden there. "I don't know. I haven't discussed it with her."

"Hmmm. And are you going to propose marriage to Abigail before this dinner party? Will she expect an announcement in front of your friends and neighbours?"

"What would be wrong with that? She would make a suitable wife. She has her father's money and let us not beat about the bush, Aunt, I could well do with an influx of capital to improve the estate, and mend the castle roof! I was up in the attics the other day and there are buckets everywhere to catch the rain coming in through the cracks."

"Indeed, money is always useful but we are talking of marriage, of giving Matilda a new mother, of giving you a wife who would work at your side. Abigail may have a lot of good qualities but she is totally wrong for Courtney."

Sir Robert crossed the room to her side. "I thought you liked her. You've known her since she was a child."

"Oh yes, Lucinda's little playmate. Always wanting what Lucinda had, even though she had no use for it. Dresses, toys, books, men. Nothing has changed."

"Aunt Honoria, you are being ridiculous. Abigail and Lucinda were the greatest of friends. She always speaks of her with much affection. She is attractive, elegant, witty"

"And yet you still hesitate."

Her nephew didn't reply. His gaze went past her, down to the headland where he could now see that his brother and daughter were making their way down the path onto the beach. Even as he watched, the figure in pale blue closed her parasol and ran after them, leaving a small slight girl in grey alone.

"All that glisters is not gold - Shakespeare can be very boring in places but I think he has the right of it in that phrase. I remember quoting it to Miss Collins not long ago. We were talking about Martin, if I recall correctly."

"Martin? So, do you think she has feelings for him?"

Lady Honoria turned back to her chair. She was very tired, the heat was proving most stressful and the stupidity of her nephew was wearisome. "Feelings for your brother? Well, who can say."

"I trust that Martin's flirting has not been misunderstood. Miss Collins is in our care."

Sharp black eyes glanced at his stern face. "Indeed she is."

"Of course, I would wish her to be happy in her future life. If marrying Martin would make her happy...." his voice trailed away and he fidgeted again with his cuff button. "Socially it would be a good match for her in many ways, but...I cannot think she would lead a happy life with my brother. Martin needs a wife who has a fortune to spend on him."

His aunt sank down in her chair and rang the bell for her maid. She was tired and wanted to sleep. She knew Robert had fancied himself in love with Lucinda, but she had watched them growing up and knew he had been dazzled by her beauty. He had thought her as beautiful in character as she was in looks. Now she could only hope that he wasn't going to be charmed yet again by appearances. She could sense a passion in him that had never been roused by his elegant wife or Abigail Richmond.

She smiled to herself as he bowed and took his leave. She had watched him grow up, seen the passionate boy and young man be beaten down by the responsibilities that surrounded him. It would take a very special young lady to free that passion. Her eyes watered and a little smile curved her lips; remembering her own youth, her own desires, her life with Pierre. As short as that had been, the explosion of their passion for each other had taken her by surprise and delight. She'd had no idea....no idea at all before her marriage.

Robert took after her in so many ways. Lady Honoria fanned herself - it was getting hotter, a storm was brewing, in more ways than one.

Sir Robert could see Catherine's slim figure at the edge of the cliff and guessed from the distant shouts and cries that the rest of the party were down at the water's edge. He slipped his hand into his pocket and fingered the ribbon that lay there. It was too late to return it to her; he had no idea why he kept it.

She turned as he got closer and he was angry to see that her eyes were full of tears. She blinked rapidly but he had seen them. Another stride took him to her side and as he glanced over the cliff, he realised why she was upset.

On the beach, Matilda was sitting watching as Martin and Bennetta paddled in the sea. Their shoes had been left higher up the beach but Martin's breeches were soaked to the knee. Bennetta was laughing, her skirts bunched up to keep them clear of the waves, her stockings wet through and clinging to her legs so that there was no doubt as to their shape. Martin was holding her arm - Sir Robert supposed it was to stop her falling - but it was an intimate picture and one that had obviously reduced Catherine to tears.

So maybe Abigail had been right all along - Catherine was growing attached to his younger brother. It was too bad of Martin to flirt with any woman who came into view and where that woman was so young and was also a Darcy of Pemberley, it was extremely unwise. Sir Robert had no doubts that Mr Darcy was not a man to be trifled with when it came to his daughter's reputation.

"Good afternoon, Miss Collins. I trust you have not been too discomforted by the heat?"

Catherine bobbed a curtsey and turned her gaze back to the trio on the beach below, checking that in their childish amusement, Martin and Bennetta were still keeping a watchful eye on Matilda. She thought Sir Robert looked hot and irritated, as if something had annoyed him. He was probably missing Abigail, she thought and tried to ignore the pain that caused her.

"No, Sir, it has been very pleasant. We have sat in the rose garden and now here on the cliff top there is always a slight breeze off the sea."

Sir Robert flung himself down on the short turf and held out his hand to help her sit by his side. "It is some time since I inspected the gardens, but I had heard that you and Matilda had been working there. I thank you for giving her something new to think about; my mother was a great lover of flowers. I would like to see more in the castle in the future."

He sighed. "I fear Abigail will find it hot and humid in Newcastle. All that way to buy a new outfit. I cannot understand you ladies sometimes. I am quite certain that Abigail has any number of dresses that would be suitable for the dance."

"Oh, I did not know the reason for Miss Richmond's journey. But then I am sure she wants to do you credit on Saturday night." Catherine did not add that she was certain that Abigail wanted a dress that would do justice to an engagement. Surely an occasion that involved friends and family would be the perfect time for them to announce their betrothal.

"It will be the first time for several years that the Courtney family has played host to its neighbours. My father did not entertain at all and I - well, I chose to lead a quiet life after Lucinda's death. I felt it kinder to Matilda to keep her quietly at home. But Abigail has persuaded me that I do Matilda a disservice by keeping her from public view. She believes that being introduced to new people will hasten her recovery, that she will have to speak eventually."

Catherine was silent. She could think of nothing encouraging to say. Abigail was wrong - of that she was certain. Being forced into company, being spoken to by people she did not know, being asked questions that demanded answers, she could only think that the child would retreat even further into silence. Which was a great shame because recently she had been convinced that the little girl was about to break her two year silence.

"You have no comment, Miss Collins?"

"I am no expert, Sir, but I do not believe that you can force her to speak."

Sir Robert sighed and fiddled with the loose button on his cuff. "That is what my brother Richard tells me. As a doctor he thinks it will happen suddenly, unexpectedly. But Abigail is buying the child a new dress in Newcastle and wants her to appear before our guests. She may be right; the noise, the colour, the music, all could stimulate her to speak."

"I will pray that it does and now, with your permission, I will call her back from the beach. The hour grows late, and it is time for her supper."

Sir Robert nodded. "I will fetch her myself and tell Martin and Miss Darcy to return to the house as well. By the way, Miss Collins, I have heard of a pony for sale locally and intend to inspect it tomorrow. Will you accompany me to the farm where it is for sale? Bessie will take care of Matilda."

Catherine felt a little skip of excitement inside her. The days until the ball were running out and once Sir Robert was engaged to Abigail there would be no chance of her spending time with him alone. She smiled up at him as he stood and held out his hand to help her to her feet. "I should be delighted. Matilda will be so pleased."

"I hope so." He stood for a moment, looking at her, as if he was going to speak, then smiled, reached out and removed the silly chain of daisies that Martin had thrown over her head. "Martin calls you the little fairy girl - perhaps that is why the flowers look happy on you." Then with a bow, he turned away and ran down the cliff steps towards the beach.

Catherine watched him go, a surge of feeling rushing through her. There was no hiding from her emotions - she loved Sir Robert Courtney - a hopeless love that burned through her like an unchecked fire. All she could hope for was that he never knew; she would be devastated if by any word or deed she let him realise her absurd feelings. He would feel pity, sorrow.

A glint on the grass caught her eye and she stooped to pick up the little button that had at last given up its struggle against Sir Robert's worrying fingers. Clasping it tightly, Catherine turned her back on the trio on the beach and began to walk back to the house. Tomorrow she would have one final day alone with him; after that, after his engagement, she would leave Courtney Castle. She had no idea where she would go, but go she must.

11

After breakfast the next morning, Bennetta knocked on the door of Sir Robert's study and entered smiling at his command. "I have come to say my goodbyes, Sir," she said, dropping him a polite curtsey. "And to thank you for your hospitality. I have written to my mama, telling her how kind you have been. I know she will be grateful."

Sir Robert looked up at the vivacious young woman standing in front of his desk, her red travelling bonnet already tied over her shining dark curls. He smiled - he didn't think there were many men in the world who would not smile at Bennetta Darcy. He pitied the young men in the future - this time next year this young woman would be a force to be reckoned with. Thank the lord he did not have to worry about Matilda in the same way just yet!

"It has been a pleasure to have your company, Miss Bennetta. And I am sure your cousin has been delighted to see you."

Bennetta's eyes gleamed and she dropped her lashes so he would not see. "I hope so. I am afraid that your brother has rather neglected her over the past few hours in his attempts to entertain me."

Sir Robert stood up abruptly, pushing his papers into disorder. "I hope Martin has not been behaving inappropriately towards either of you. Sometimes he jokes and young ladies think he is serious and..."

Bennetta raised a hand, deciding that a little jealousy was a good thing but too much could only cause more problems. She liked Martin and was quite sure that he liked her and would be fun to flirt with. And another thing she was sure of was that he had no warm feelings for Catherine.

They had spoken together when they were playing on the beach with Matilda and had both voiced similar opinions as to where her cousin's heart lay. Martin had also made it clear that he thought his brother's feelings were equally fixed, although Bennetta was not quite as sure. She recognised the power of a woman such as Abigail Richmond.

"On my word, Mr Martin has been the perfect gentleman. We are the greatest of friends. As for his feelings for my cousin, I refuse to gossip. Let us just say that I am only sorry I cannot stay for your dinner party and the entertainment afterwards. Up in Scotland, the dancing is very different. And one day I may even grow to love the sound of the bagpipes, but I fear that day is some way off still! I am sure we shall meet again, Sir Robert. Perhaps in Derbyshire when you next visit Richard and Cassandra, and your dear sister, too, of course."

"Or you could break your journey traveling back south when you leave Scotland."

Bennetta shook her head. "Well, I might, if Catherine is still here. But I have been told that you are to marry again soon and then, of course, she will seek a new employment as she would not be needed, unless her affections were won by someone living in the area."

Sir Robert frowned and Bennetta wondered if she had gone too far. It was rather like poking a sleeping lion with a stick - amusing but dangerous,

"Surely Miss Collins will not be needing any further employment? She is here as my guest, not as a servant. If she leaves Courtney, surely she will return to her parents' home in Hertfordshire."

Bennetta widened her eyes and managed to look very young and innocent. "Oh dear, I do hope I have not given away any secrets. It's just that Catherine mentioned just as we were retiring for bed last night that her stepmother suggests she look elsewhere to live. I suppose Longbourn is a very small house - well, in comparison to Pemberley, that is."

Sir Robert was silent as he escorted her to the door. "I will write to your father, telling him you left us in good spirits. Ah, here is your cousin, looking for you, no doubt. And dressed for riding." He raised an eyebrow in astonishment to see Catherine wearing a dark amber hued riding habit. He had expected her to join him dressed in the dark blue serge skirt and jacket she had worn before. He realised he was staring, but couldn't tear his gaze away from the amber hat with a curved feather that swept round her face to just under her chin.

"My mama sent the habit," Bennetta said carelessly. "She was certain my cousin did not take one with her when she travelled north. And Catherine tells me you are to ride out today to buy a pony for Matilda."

"Indeed and I...I must go and change myself. I will see you in the stable yard, Miss Collins."

Bennetta watched him walk away and then turned, smiling at the expression on her cousin's face. "I think Sir Robert found your new outfit most pleasing!"

"Oh, don't be such a silly, Bennetta. He is probably just glad I will not shame him whilst in his company this morning."

Bennetta linked their arms as they left the castle and walked across the courtyard to the stable block. The sun was beating down again, another hot day was on its way, although there was a stillness to the air which foretold of a storm coming. The Pemberley coach was waiting, one groom already seated on the box, the other holding the horses' heads.

Bennetta's maid was being helped up into the carriage by Donald who held the door open for her mistress.

Bennetta hugged Catherine warmly. "Oh, I shall miss you. It has been so lovely to see you and to meet Matilda and Mr Martin and Sir Robert, too, of course. You do like him, don't you Catherine?"

"Mr Martin is a charming boy," she replied, willfully misunderstanding.

Dark eyes gleamed - "Oh yes, charming. Sir Robert - well, that's not a word you could use about him, is it?"

"Sir Robert has a far better character than his brother!" Catherine retaliated hotly, then realised she had been tricked into showing far more of her feelings than was seemly.

"So, you like Mr Martin, but you care more for Sir Robert?"

Catherine tried to keep her voice light and playful, replying in the same tone as that her cousin was using, but it was to no avail. She couldn't speak of how she felt and, to her horror, she felt tears brimming in her eyes.

"Oh Catherine, I am sorry! I have upset you. Pay me no attention. I am young and silly and should not be allowed out in adult company. Well, that's what Anne says! Look, the horses are growing impatient. I must go."

She allowed Donald to hand her up into the carriage and pulled down the window to speak as the big coach began to move slowly through the yard. "Write to me, Catherine. Tell me all about the dinner party. And tell me if he...." But the rest of her words were lost in the sound of the many hooves on the cobbles and then there was just a handkerchief waving from the window and then Bennetta was gone.

An hour later, three riders crested a hill and pulled their mounts to a halt, giving them time to catch their breath after the steep climb.

Catherine allowed Sir Robert to help her from the saddle and pass the reins of their horses to the groom who had accompanied them.

She had enjoyed the ride, glorying in the rush of fresh air in her face, the strength of the animal beneath her. The grey mare was an easy horse but a gallant one, covering the rough ground easily. She was well aware that Sir Robert was keeping a firm check on his horse; it was a far more powerful animal and would have soon out run her mare.

Standing together, they stared out over the lonely countryside, larks spiralling up into the hot sky, curlews crying as they flirted across the surface of the moorland. Sir Robert pointed with his whip.

"We are heading for that farm down in the valley, Miss Collins. The owner breeds horses and I am reliably told has a very nice Fell pony mare for sale. Five years old, easy to handle. Everything that a young girl could want, but I need to see the animal go through its paces before I decide. And, of course, I want your opinion as well."

Catherine looked up at him, startled, unaware how pretty she looked under the riding hat with its curling feather. "I am no judge of horses, Sir Robert. If it has a kind face and a velvety nose, then that will be enough for me."

Sir Robert gave a great shout of laughter. "Would you choose your future husband from the same requirements? A kind face I can understand but a velvety nose might prove a problem."

She laughed, feeling the hot colour creep up into her cheeks. There was only one man she would ever choose to be her husband and he was far, far beyond her reach.

A silence fell between them and then Sir Robert said, "Miss Bennetta mentioned to me that your family feel you would be better off employed out in the world rather than living at home. She says that you will look for a post elsewhere."

"Bennetta had no right to talk of my personal affairs."

"I have the feeling that Miss Darcy cares not a jot who and what she talks about. Matilda will be very sad if you leave Courtney."

'And you?' she thought, her heart racing. 'Will you be sad if I go? No, for by then you will have married Abigail Richmond.'

"It distresses me greatly to think of upsetting Matilda."

"Then perhaps you should decide to stay."

She looked up to find him gazing at her, his eyes dark, frowning as if angry. Perhaps he was. Newly married people did not want to have the bother of caring for a child, of making day to day decisions about her education and well-being. Catherine had convinced herself that Abigail would not want her to remain at the castle, but maybe she had been wrong. She knew he loved Matilda deeply, but a new wife, especially a woman like Abigail, would need all his attention and it would obviously be better if he knew his daughter was in the care of someone he could trust.

Sir Robert's fingers tightened on the red ribbon he now carried everywhere in his pocket. His feelings for Catherine were getting deeper and stronger with every passing day. But she had given him no indication that she felt anything for him at all. He was just Matilda's father, her host at Courtney Castle. If he declared himself and she rejected him, then she would definitely leave. There was no way she would remain under his roof. If he could persuade her to stay, then perhaps she would grow to care for him.

Catherine fingered the little shirt button that she carried in the pocket of her riding habit. A silly little token but one she treasured. Her mind was in a whirl. For Matilda's sake, could she stay once he married Abigail? Was she that brave? Or that foolish?

"I will think about it, Sir," she whispered and with a brief nod, he helped her back into the saddle and swinging up onto his own horse, led the way down the hillside towards the farm.

Catherine could hardly concentrate as she was introduced to the owner of the farm, Mr Scarne, a big, bluff man with the same broad accent as Bessie and Donald. She shook his hand, smiled and hoped he didn't realise that she didn't understand one in three words of what was obviously a warm welcome.

He led her to where a bale of hay had been placed at the side of the field and she sat, watching, as the pony was led out and trotted round to show off its paces. Sir Robert watched every movement, stripping off his riding jacket in the heat of the day to examine the mare in detail, running his hands down her legs, checking on everything he could think of to make sure that this pony was ideal for his daughter.

Catherine nodded when asked a question and tried to seem intelligent but she was so bedazzled by the heat and shaken by Sir Robert's request that she remained at Courtney that she knew she must appear a very stupid girl indeed. Surely, he must understand that her position at Courtney would not be his alone to decide. When he married, Abigail would be in charge of the overall running of the castle and have a great say in what happened to Matilda.

She frowned as she watched the two men examining the pony. Last night Bessie had told her that Abigail had taken to coming into Matilda's room when the child had gone to bed and Catherine had gone downstairs for dinner. There was nothing wrong with that, of course, but Bessie had seemed upset and doubtful.

"She keeps on at the child about her ma. On and on - how lovely she was, how much Miss Matilda must miss her. I just don't reckon it be right, Miss Collins. I don't want her to forget her ma, but harking back to the past, telling her how she doesn't know how she can be so brave, I don't like to hear that."

She had hesitated, then burst out, "And last night I overheard her saying that perhaps Matilda would be happier living far away from where her ma died. That she would find it easier. I reckon she wants to send little miss away once she marries Sir Robert."

Catherine had tried to calm the nursemaid down. There was no way she was going to gossip with Bessie about Abigail, and after all, what had she done that was so bad? Reminded Matilda of how lovely her mother had been? She needed little reminding; the portrait in the drawing-room must have told her that every time she looked at it.

Catherine sighed now, watching Sir Robert, admiring the way he stood and moved. Could he really be so blind as not to see that Abigail resented any reminder of Lucinda, that she would be far happier when Matilda was sent away to an establishment of some sort that cared for children with afflictions?

At last Sir Robert and Mr Scarne began to talk about money - there was obviously to be a great deal of bargaining - and thinking it only polite to leave the men to their financial arrangements, she wandered across to the stables.

Sir Robert watched her go, wondering not for the first time how someone so slight and small could make such an impression.

Mr Scarne followed his gaze and said warmly, "Wife and I was made up to hear you'll be wed again soon, Sir Robert. Pretty young maid, too, if you'll forgive my saying. And a sensible one, from all the wife's heard locally, even if she doesn't come from these parts. Make a fine Lady Courtney."

"Miss Collins? Oh, no, she's......" He stopped abruptly because he knew, without a doubt, that was what he wanted. Catherine wasn't the elegant, beautiful wife he'd imagined he needed, but he knew she had brought love and the joy of living back into his humdrum existence. And he also had to admit that the feelings he had had as a young man for Lucinda paled into insignificance compared to the fire that burned through him every time he looked at Catherine.

Finally, the deal for the pony was settled by a handshake and refusing the farmer's offer of refreshment, Sir Robert headed for the stables to find Catherine while Mr Scarne returned to his house to make out a receipt. The sun blazed down on his bare head and he felt dizzy with the roar of emotions inside him.

The stables were large and dim, smelling sweetly of hay with the tang of horses and leather. Catherine sighed; she felt dizzy and it was wonderful to be sheltered from the sun. Most of the occupants were out in the fields and only a very elderly Shire horse, grey around the muzzle, remained comfortably in his stall. His head appeared over his half door as she walked towards him, dark eyes looking at her curiously. A sack of carrots stood open and she took out two and offered them, the big head drooping down to snuffle the treats from her palm.

Catherine rubbed her hand down the long nose, smiling a little as she remembered Sir Robert's laughter at her comment earlier. When he smiled, when he laughed, he seemed a different person and for one minute she gloried in the fact that she had never seen him laugh with Abigail. He often smiled at her, but they were the smiles of an affectionate friend and not...

"Catherine!"

She spun round in alarm; Sir Robert was standing close behind her, in her daydreaming she hadn't heard him enter the stables. She gasped and took a step back and in a second, the great Shire horse had lifted the amber velvet hat off her head and stood chewing it, the feather sticking out of his mouth. As he'd snatched off the hat, he'd pushed her forward; several of the pins holding her hair came loose and she stumbled towards Sir Robert with her bright brown hair beginning to tumble down over her shoulders, her eyes full of laughter.

"Catherine!" His voice was rough and as he reached out with one hand to grasp her waist, the other tangled in her hair as he bent his head towards her, as if he were going to kiss her, their lips no more than an inch apart.

Time seemed to stand still and then he was stepping back, closing his eyes as if in pain and muttering words she didn't know under his breath. Then there were voices and the farmer and the groom appeared in the stable doorway, leading the little pony.

The ride home was made in complete silence. They no longer rode side by side: Sir Robert spurred on ahead and Catherine was left to canter along with the groom leading the pony beside her. She was aware of the sun beating down on her bare head, her hair now completely loose and flying in the breeze. But she didn't care. She was confused, elated, frightened and angry all at the same time. How dare he try to kiss her? She had done nothing to encourage him. How could he possibly think she was the type of girl who would let a man kiss her? What should she do?

There had been no time to remonstrate, or even laugh as if it had been some silly joke that she could pass off with a shrug of her shoulders. But what was upsetting her so much - fingers tangling in her hair as if he would never let her go, his hand, warm and hard against her waist and....

She tried to stop her thoughts but they were merciless - she had not pulled away, she had done nothing to stop him. Could he possibly think she had stepped towards him on purpose? That she had asked for his kiss? And she knew with a dreadful certainty that if he had kissed her, she would have returned his embrace. What would he say to her? What could he say?

He was waiting when she finally trotted into the stable yard, but he was not alone, his brother was there to welcome Abigail whose carriage had obviously just arrived as she was dressed for travelling, looking cool and elegant. She was laughing with the Courtney brothers, pointing out a pile of parcels and boxes that her maid and a footman were carrying into the castle.

"I have bought the most divine dress for Matilda to wear for the ball. I know you will wish to introduce her to your guests before dinner and I must admit, Robert, that her wardrobe is sadly lacking for a young lady of her breeding and station in life. I'm surprised that Miss Collins has not thought to say so. Oh - !"

She turned in astonishment as Catherine reined to a halt and Martin caught hold of the horse's reins and helped her to dismount. Abigail stared - she hardly recognised the girl - hatless, tangles of bright brown hair, cascading to her shoulders, she was dusty and grimy and even had what looked like straw in her hair, as if she had been leaning against a haystack. But above all, she had a high colour and looked suddenly very pretty.

Abigail cast a quick look at Robert and was relieved to see that he didn't seem impressed. He was frowning heavily, all his attention on the new pony. She wasn't surprised; no gentleman liked to be seen out riding with a woman without a hat, her hair loose and windblown.

"La, Miss Collins, what a state you are in, to be sure," she said lightly. "Did you have a fall? You seem to have lost your hat."

"We have had a very busy day," Sir Robert said before Catherine could reply. "Here is Matilda's surprise pony."

"A nice animal." Martin's sharp gaze went from his brother to Catherine and back again. "She will be delighted, I'm sure. I take it you paid a good price for the creature."

"A heavy price," Sir Robert said shortly and glanced across at Catherine, but she was busy trying to brush the worst of the dust from her skirts and didn't notice the pain in his eyes.

But Martin did. He chatted on blithely as he escorted Abigail back inside the castle, but his mind was busy. His brother was not a man who showed his feelings easily, but there had been no mistaking the look on his face when Catherine had trotted into the yard, the sun catching all the bright chestnuts and bronzes in her brown hair. It was the face of a man in love, even though he had quickly hidden behind one of his usual frowns.

"Do you think they have had an argument," he murmured to Abigail as they passed into the south hall.

"Who?"

"Robert and little Miss Collins, of course."

Abigail raised her eyebrows at him. "She may have displeased him in some way. Perhaps she was flirting with one of the farm hands."

Martin burst out laughing. "Oh Abigail, I think you are far from the truth of the matter. Have you not seen the way he looks at her? The way she looks at him when she doesn't think anyone will notice? No, their appearance and demeanor made me think they have had a lovers' quarrel."

Abigail's steps faltered for a second and then she swept on. "What nonsense you do talk, Martin. Miss Collins is, no doubt, a very worthy young woman but surely she would not think of becoming Lady Courtney! It is a ridiculous idea. Why, Robert is as good as engaged to me."

"But he hasn't asked for your hand yet, has he?"

Abigail's lips tightened and she glanced round to make sure none of the servants were within hearing distance. "I am quite convinced he is waiting for the day of the dinner party. He will no doubt ask me before the guests arrive and announce it after dinner when we begin the dancing."

"That's a very pretty picture, my dear, but will Robert act the role you have given him in your little play? Don't forget, Catherine is at least ten years younger than you, pretty, sensible and already a great friend of Matilda's. And Robert needs an heir. I need Robert to get an heir, if I'm honest! Can you imagine me having to live up here in the wilds of Northumberland if anything should happen to him?"

"I am quite capable of producing a child!"

"Ah, but what if it is another girl? I somehow can't see you trying year after year for a boy! Living here, isolated when the snow comes, no society, no gaiety, just - "

"Stop! This is all nonsense. I refuse to listen. Miss Collins is not going to marry Robert and I am. You forget, Martin, that I bring more to this union than the chance of an heir. Whatever charms Miss Collins may have, she lacks the one thing I have plenty of - money! And once we are wed, I will persuade him to employ a useful steward to take care of all the boring estate business and we can then spend most of our time in London. Don't forget, I already have a house in Grosvenor Street."

Martin nodded, not wanting to argue, but he wondered how this intelligent woman could so wrongly read his brother's character. All the money in the world would not tear him away from Courtney.

Outside in the sunlit stable yard, Catherine waited in some trepidation for Sir Robert to speak to her, but he did not. As usual as soon as he arrived home, people were wanting his attention, asking for orders, reporting on their duties, the work they had undertaken that day, hopeful that he could sort out a million and one problems that had occurred in the daily running of the big estate.

She watched as Donald appeared, touched his hand to his forehead and took the little pony away, with instructions on washing and grooming, getting her ready to give to Matilda on her birthday. Finally, Catherine knew she could wait no longer and why should she; 'I am not a servant girl' she thought angrily, 'even if he did mistake me for one when we first met.'

She turned to go when at last he spoke, his voice cold and harsh. "Miss Collins, Catherine, there is no time to speak now. My behaviour was inexcusable but I hope we can talk privately very soon."

She dropped him a short curtsey. "As you wish, Sir."

He raked his fingers through his dark hair at her distant tone. "There is no time with this wretched party almost upon us. Will you do me the courtesy of waiting until it is over before we speak?"

Catherine swallowed hard, fighting back tears: refused to cry in front of him. It seemed plain to her that although he had apologised, her continued presence at Courtney would disturb him and remind him of a moment he would rather forget. How annoyed he must be now for having asked her earlier to consider staying at the castle. Obviously, he did not want her to leave before the party, with all the extra work that would entail for everyone caring for Matilda, but she was quite convinced that their conversation afterwards would be to arrange the earliest date for her removal from his life altogether.

12

The rest of the day passed far too slowly for Catherine's peace of mind. Matilda was crotchety because she had been forced to amuse herself indoors all morning under Mrs Crawford's watchful eye when she wanted to play in the rose garden. Bessie had twisted her ankle very badly, chasing the little girl down the spiral staircase; she could hardly walk and had been told to stay in bed, resting.

Catherine was only too aware that Sir Robert did not want his daughter wandering around the stables and perhaps discovering her pony before her birthday, so she put on a very old grey dress that had seen better days and took Matilda down to the beach. Her spirits rose a little as they walked along the low tide line: she loved this part of the estate so much. There was a freedom in walking by the sea that you never found in the quiet sedate lanes of Hertfordshire.

The sea was flat and blue and the sun still beat down, making them glad of their bonnets, and Matilda's bad mood began to pass as she danced around, collecting shells and streams of seaweed.

Catherine wondered how long this hot weather would last: surely it must rain very soon. The air was heavy and sultry and although there were no clouds at the moment, she felt that somewhere over the far horizon, a storm was lurking.

They finally reached the outcrop of rocks that separated the Courtney beach from the stretch of coast where the caves were hollowed out of the cliffs. Matilda pulled at Catherine's hand, her eyes pleading for them to go further.

Catherine shook her head. "No, the tide is turning and swiftly, too. Look, those rock pools are already filling with water. It isn't safe, Matilda." She would have liked to have added that perhaps they could adventure further on another day, but she wasn't at all sure she would be living at Courtney for much longer and she hated to make a promise to the child that she could not keep.

With Bessie unable to take charge of bath and bedtime, Catherine was only too pleased to do so. She sent word that she would eat her dinner early with Matilda, thankful that at least she would not have to face Sir Robert over the table. When supper was over and the little girl washed and dressed for sleep, she sat by her bed, reading a fairy story to her, glad of these peaceful moments they could share together.

She had just closed the book and pulled a light quilt over the child's shoulders as she snuggled down to sleep when the door opened and Abigail came in. Catherine swung round, finger to lips, but it was too late, Matilda sat upright in bed, her eyes wide.

"La Miss Collins, I have disturbed you at your duties, but I am sure Matilda will not object to staying awake a little longer. Listen, child, I have bought you a beautiful dress to wear tomorrow night. I know your dear papa wishes you to look your very best in front of his company. I will take you downstairs to give your curtsey to the guests and I want you to try your hardest to answer their kind questions and not continue with this silly nonsense of not speaking."

She crossed to the bed, stroking back the long fair hair that fell into Matilda's eyes. "Such a dear, sweet child. So like your sainted mama. Why, here is the miniature of her by your bedside. I know you will never forget her with that to remind you every night. But I am sure you will be delighted when your papa marries and gives you another mother. Even perhaps one who knew Lucinda Courtney well."

Matilda frowned and reached out to take back the miniature. For a second Catherine thought Abigail was going to chastise the child for snatching, but she just laughed lightly and turned away from the bed.

"I must not detain you from your work, Miss Collins, I have the dress in my room and will send my maid for Matilda tomorrow evening. It is safer in my care, I would not want it creased or dirtied."

Catherine nodded and expected her to leave but instead, she walked through the door into the day nursery and Catherine could do no more than to follow.

"You are obviously not eating with us this evening," Abigail said, looking distastefully at the remains of their supper still on the table.

"No, not this evening, you see Bessie, the nurserymaid - "

"La, do not bother me with such domesticities, dear Miss Collins. I leave all that to those of you whose job it is. Indeed, I think it is always the best of situations if everyone accepts the position in life they have and do not aspire to anything different." She walked across to the window and stood fanning herself. "Goodness, when will this heat end? I declare I am quite fatigued."

"Surely we should all try to better ourselves in life."

Abigail laughed. "Oh that is a very progressive thought indeed. But when you interfere with the established way of life then you can do more harm than good."

Catherine remained silent.

"For example, I have heard a rumour - a silly one but rumours do spread - that you have plans to become Lady Courtney." She held up a hand as Catherine began to reply, "Oh, I know it is a most scandalous falsehood, my dear, and one to which I would not give a moment's consideration, but it is one that could do Robert a great deal of harm. Gossip linking him to a young lady who is living under his roof would be most distasteful. And, as we are to announce our engagement tomorrow night, you can see that I too find talk of such an alliance almost unbearable to hear."

"Miss Richmond, I have no idea where you heard this rumour but let me assure you that I have never aspired to become Lady Courtney!"

Abigail sighed. "Oh indeed, I have every confidence in your common-sense, Miss Collins. Indeed, Robert told me that that was one of the most important things he listed when asking Mrs Darcy for her help in finding a governess for Matilda. You do not have to apologise to me but the gossip - a young girl working here, not quite a servant, not quite one of the family..."

Catherine took a deep breath, anger beginning to thread through her. "If, as you say, you are about to become engaged to Sir Robert, I cannot imagine any circumstance where he would ask me to be his wife. Or any circumstance where the gossip could possibly be true."

"Well, as to that, Robert has a very highly developed conscience. You both seemed very disturbed when you returned with the pony. I am wondering if he might have said or done something whilst the two of you were alone that might have been misconstrued by your good self. And he would then feel honour bound to propose marriage rather than be labelled a cad and a scoundrel."

Catherine realised that she had been clenching her fists so hard that her nails were biting into her flesh. She was hot with mortification. Abigail's words could only be taken one way - that Sir Robert had discussed with her what had occurred in the stables that morning. Oh, the thought was unbearable, she would not have believed he could have talked about such a personal moment to someone else.

Abigail was well aware of her companion's distress; her cheeks were flushed and she was obviously fighting back tears. So Martin had been right! Something had occurred this morning whilst Robert and the governess were out buying the pony. Perhaps he hadn't proposed, but some sort of advance might have been made. She had been right to confront Catherine this evening, to stop this before it went any further.

But she knew she must tread carefully; she did not want to alienate the girl so much that she left Courtney too promptly. She was, after all, a distant relation to the Darcys of Pemberley and although Abigail had never met them, they were one of the most important families in the land and she did not want to antagonise them in any way.

She sighed and held out her hand to Catherine. "My dear, you are so young, perhaps you do not yet realise that your reputation must always be beyond reproach as far as society is aware. Although, of course, any girl would be flattered to receive any attention from a man of consequence such as Robert."

"Sir Robert has always been kind and considerate towards me," Catherine managed to say.

"Oh, I am certain of that. Kindness is such a large part of his nature and sometimes I know that he can say thingswhich people might well misinterpret as something else .. But as you know, our engagement is at hand and I know Robert is delighted at the thought of our union and, of course, the funds that I will be bringing to the marriage."

She laughed lightly. "Courtney Castle is in need of a substantial amount of money, as I am sure you are aware. Robert has been driven almost to distraction by lack of funds. Well, those days are almost over."

"And is the engagement to be announced tomorrow?" Catherine was fighting to hide her feelings: she refused to let this vain, arrogant woman see how much distress she was causing. Her fingers closed over the silly little shirt button that she kept in her pocket and remembered once again the warmth of his hand on her waist.

Abigail smiled, as if she had a big secret she couldn't tell. "Well, let us wait and see! I can say no more, but would suggest that you plan on leaving Courtney some time in the autumn. I never believe in long engagements, do you?" With the briefest nod, she swept out of the room, leaving Catherine shaken and deeply unhappy.

The next morning dawned to overcast skies. It was still warm but the clouds out to sea over the horizon were dark. Catherine had lain awake most of the night, and felt heavy eyed and tired.

Tossing and turning, she had gone over and over the events inside the stable but was no clearer in understanding Sir Robert's behaviour or her own. The look on his face, the expression in his eyes all told her one thing, that he cared for her. But his tone of voice and angry demeanour when they arrived home told her another, that he was ashamed both of his behaviour and hers.

Burning through her mind was the thought that he had told Abigail what had occurred. How else would she have known? How could he have divulged something so private to a third party, even someone he was apparently about to marry? That was not the act of a gentleman although instinctively she knew he was one of the most honorable men she had ever met. But Abigail had known!

Drearily she washed and dressed; at least this torture would soon be over. Tonight, the engagement would be announced and she could make her plans to leave Courtney. She decided she would go back to Pemberley and beg Cousin Elizabeth to find her a situation in that neighbourhood. There was no way she could return to Longbourn and if she worked in Derbyshire, then there would be a chance to meet up with Bennetta on occasion.

Sir Robert had said he wanted to talk to her when the ball was over. Well, tomorrow was Matilda's birthday so it was unlikely there would be a good opportunity until all that excitement was over as well, but the day after that would come soon enough. She was quite sure that their talk would concern the date of her departure.

She had hoped to spend a quiet morning with Matilda but today of all days, the usually docile little girl had decided to be naughty. Mrs Crawford had sent Peggy, one of the youngest maids to help

Catherine as Bessie was still unable to walk, and Catherine, hearing her voice raised in exasperation, had gone through into the night nursery to find Matilda jumping on her bed and refusing to get dressed.

Even though peace and quiet was all she wanted, Catherine had to admit smiling a little. This was the sort of normal naughtiness that every small child exhibited at times and over the past few weeks she had found it sadly lacking in Matilda. Was this a sign that she was at last coming out of the odd state of mind she had been in since her mother's death? Perhaps it would be this evening that she would talk once more. She prayed fervently that it was so.

At last she managed to get Matilda washed and dressed but once downstairs, she pulled a face at her porridge, refused to make honey rivers and sat crumbling her bread into little pellets to line up around the edge of her plate.

Luckily because they were so late, the breakfast room was empty. Catherine felt relief; she was dreading facing Sir Robert today and was in no mood for a flirtation with Martin or barbed comments from Abigail. She was wearily trying to make Matilda sit still and finish her milk when Mrs Crawford came in, hesitating as if she wished to speak.

It was not Mrs Crawford's place to criticize her betters, but she had to admit she had never taken to Miss Richmond when she was young and hadn't changed her opinion now that lady had reached the age of thirty. It had been obvious that she had always wanted to marry Robert Courtney and Mrs Crawford had a vivid memory of her face as she left the church following his marriage to Lucinda.

The servants had been sitting in the back pews and had had a clear view of everyone as they paraded down the aisle. Miss Richmond had been trying to laugh and smile and join in the festivities, but it had all been an act and her anger at being overlooked had shown through.

Well it certainly looked as if she was going to win her prize at last, but as far as Mrs Crawford was concerned there was a vast gap between wanting to be Lady Courtney and taking on all the responsibilities of that role.

Mrs Crawford was worried about the evening's events - the first social occasion at Courtney for years. Cook was coping well with all the different dishes that were required for the dinner, although she had had to send as far as Newcastle for some of the ingredients. But the sudden heatwave was causing havoc with the iced and jellied dishes; none of them would set properly and there were worries about the cream turning sour.

No, it was the appearance of the rooms that were the housekeeper's great concern. She had set the maids to work polishing the long dining table until it gleamed; all the rugs had been taken up and beaten. But the room was still dark and gloomy and even fetching out the solid silver candelabra from the storeroom had done nothing to lighten its appearance.

The keys to the ballroom had eventually been found - on a hook in the scullery - and work was already underway on cleaning and polishing the floor, finding the chalk to rub in to prevent dancers slipping, stopping up the mouse holes - she must remember to shut the castle cat into the room for a couple of hours - and fitting new beeswax candles in all the many sconces on the walls. Tallow wouldn't do - they smelt dreadful. But there were still a great many details that needed decisions and she was reluctant to go ahead without permission from someone in the family.

She had spoken to Miss Richmond; as acting hostess she was responsible but that lady had not wanted to be concerned with the boring household aspect of the party. She had just told Mrs Crawford to do what she wanted but to make sure the musicians arrived in time and were ready to play for dancing after dinner. Which was all good and well, but...

..."You see, Miss Collins, the dining-room looks cold and bare, even with the table laid with our best Wedgewood dinner service. I would not wish for Sir Robert's guests to think that we are proving less than hospitable or that - " she paused, then went on meaningly, "that Courtney is low on funds."

Catherine understood what she meant: if rumours spread that the estate was short of money, that bills would not be paid, then it could cause Sir Robert great harm. She had never truly understood credit, why people such as the Courtneys, the Darcys, why even her own mother, never paid their bills outright, but had accounts that they settled in part or in whole whenever they chose to do so. She had noticed that Mr Scarne, the farmer, had obviously wanted to be paid in guineas for the pony, which she thought a very sensible arrangement.

"I did think of getting down from the attics those old tapestries that used to hang on the dining-room walls. Sir Edgar had them packed away when Lady Courtney died. But I have no idea of the state they're in and we haven't got the time to have them repaired if the moth have been busy."

"Sir Edgar did not care for them?"

Mrs Crawford frowned. "I think it was all the colour, Miss. And the happy pictures of young lovers, unicorns, forests and fairies. They reminded him too much of what he had lost. He wanted the castle to be dark, as if in continual mourning."

Catherine sighed: she could see her quiet morning, nursing her headache and trying not to think about Robert, vanishing into the distance. She sent Matilda upstairs, saying that it would be kind to visit Bessie, telling her that there would be no lessons today, and as the child scampered happily away, she accompanied Mrs Crawford into the dining-room.

Under the great black beams that criss-crossed the ceiling, the table shone, the silver candelabra glittered and the place settings gleamed with the best dinner service, freshly washed and polished. Although it was morning, the grey skies outside gave little light through the small mullioned windows.

"To be sure it is not the most cheerful room I have ever been in," Catherine said, "but with the candles and lamps lit and the colours of the ladies' gowns it will look very different. I would suggest you get some men to take away that old tree trunk in the fireplace because all it ever does is smoulder and build a good fire with dry logs. I know it is still warm today, but by this evening it will no doubt be cooler and the light from it will be cheerful and welcoming."

She stared round, seeking more inspiration. "Flowers!" she said suddenly, remembering the dining-room at Pemberley, the exquisite arrangements on tall carved pedestals, white and pink and red. "We need vases of flowers in here, Mrs Crawford. Pale colours, white and yellow and pink, to show up against the grey walls."

Mrs Crawford nodded, her eyes gleaming. It was a long time since flowers had been picked for decoration but now that Miss Collins had mentioned them, she could see they would make a great difference to the look of the room. "But do we have flowers in the garden, Miss? Ones that will do us credit."

Catherine smiled. "Matilda and I have been working hard in the flower garden. I know there are enough trailing roses to make a show."

"Lady Courtney was fond of that old flower garden. Sir Edgar used to have a quick temper and I know she escaped there to find some peace and quiet! It's nice to see Miss Matilda liking the flowers, too."

"She has neat fingers and is patient, which is rare in a child. She realises that the tiny seeds will not bloom overnight and doesn't insist on digging them up to check on their progress as my own little sister does at home!"

Mrs Crawford smiled, then said, "Miss Richmond's orders are for the musicians to sit at the end of the room, to play softly during dinner."

Catherine looked at her doubtfully. "They will be very close to the guests; there will hardly be room for the servants to pass round the table." She made up her mind. Abigail could well be annoyed but she was past caring. "It is going to be a warm night. I do not think it will rain until tomorrow. Place them outside on the pathway. With the windows open we will be able to hear them easily and they will not be underfoot."

"An excellent plan!" She spun round to find Martin standing in the doorway, smiling at her. "I'm fond of music but it is hard to talk to your dinner partner when some great fellow is playing a violin right next to your ear. Of course, when I think of you, Miss Collins, I think of you dancing. Why that was what you were doing when we first met. I shall expect you to save me several dances tonight. Perhaps you can teach me how to be as light on my feet as you are, fairy girl!"

Catherine found herself smiling at his nonsense. "I am sure you will be able to find partners far more adept than I, Sir."

"Oh adept - I have no time for adept! Abigail will be adept, every step, every turn beautifully executed, but if I have to sit through a dinner and evening with the good, solid people who are coming tonight, I want, nay, I need, a little magic from my dance partner."

He escorted her back into the hall. "Where are you off to now, fairy girl?"

"We need flowers, lots of flowers, for the dining-room."

"Well then, I shall offer you my arm and help you search in the gardens, although I warn you, I am not brave where bees and beetles are concerned. I may scream and run away, leaving you to fight the battle of the roses all on your own."

Catherine accepted his arm and found herself smiling as they left the castle and headed for the gardens. Martin was amusing, uncomplicated company, his flirtation balm to a soul that was sore and troubled by the overwhelming feelings she had for his brother. She didn't need to guard every word she said or be careful not to accidentally touch his hand when they were picking flowers.

Eventually Martin tired of what had now become a chore and, kissing her hand in a gallant fashion, said he would walk across to the stables and check on Matilda's pony. "I admit I am looking forward to seeing the child's face tomorrow, but not as much as I am looking forward to dancing with you tonight, fairy girl! Don't let my big brother mark your card for too many."

Catherine found herself blushing and buried her face in the soft petals of the bouquet she was holding. Ten minutes later she had filled two baskets with flowers and was about to leave the garden when voices stopped her. She looked up to find Sir Robert and Abigail Richmond standing in the doorway to the walled garden. He was looking round, his usually stern face softened by a smile.

"My mother had this area walled in and planted to provide flowers for the castle and Susannah, my sister, loved to sit in here and read, I recall. It was Susannah who made the little herb garden but since she left to live with Richard, no one has cared for it."

Catherine returned his smile and for a moment she met his gaze before turning away, aware that hot colour was flooding her cheeks. "Matilda and I often work out here. For a young child she is good at sketching flowers and she loves watching the birds."

"I have seen you both here. You looked - happy." There was a silence as his dark blue eyes gleamed and seemed to ask her a question.

"La, Miss Collins, surely you could have asked one of the gardeners to cut flowers for you," Abigail said, breaking the silence and altering the angle of her parasol so she could stand closer to Sir Robert. "Your dress is all over dirt and those green stains will be so hard to get out."

"It is nothing that won't wash off," Catherine said, fighting to keep her composure. "And the flowers are needed urgently to decorate the great hall before this evening. Mr Martin has been helping me but has just left to check on Matilda's pony."

Sir Robert found he was crushing the ribbon he carried in his pocket. So his brother had been here, picking flowers with Catherine, flirting with her no doubt, to bring that pink flush into her cheeks. He had never before considered himself a jealous man, but now he wished Martin to go to the devil and the sooner the better.

"And Matilda? Surely she should be your priority and not - flowers." The words were out before he could stop them and, to his horror, he saw a flash of hurt cross her face.

"Oh Robert, you are so harsh!" Abigail smiled and tapped him on the arm. "I am quite sure that Matilda is being well looked after by other members of the staff."

"She has gone to visit Bessie who is still confined to her room with a bad ankle. I am sure Matilda is quite safe; she will be sitting listening to stories of mermaids and emerald caves."

Abigail frowned and pouted. "Really Robert, I do think the child shows an unhealthy interest in all these old stories. She needs strict schooling in other subjects which will be of use to her as she grows older. Let me tell you again about this school I have heard of in York; it has such a good reputation with afflicted children."

"Yes, yes, so you have said before. Miss Collins - let me call a gardener to carry those flowers back to the castle."

Catherine shook her head. "No, Sir, that will not be necessary. I need to get them into water as soon as possible, so I will hurry back. Please do not disturb your walk. Do not disturb yourselves in any fashion." She dropped a brief curtsey and turned away, seeking refuge away from his challenging blue gaze.

"Oh Miss Collins, don't forget I shall be sending my maid for Matilda this evening. Robert, you will be delighted to see her in the dress I have bought her."

"I look forward to seeing all you ladies in your finery."

"La, Robert! Don't embarrass poor Miss Collins so. She might not have travelled north with a suitable evening dress as she is just here to care for Matilda for a few months. I'm sure the question of grand entertainment was never discussed. Indeed, would you care to eat upstairs with Matilda, Miss Collins? The last thing Robert would want is to cause you distress in any fashion."

Catherine forced herself to relax her grip on the flowers she was holding; they were in danger of being crushed.

"Thank you for your concern, Miss Richmond," she said quietly. "I will eat downstairs. It will be interesting to meet neighbours and friends of the family. Now, if you will excuse me..." And she turned and hurried away, trying not to hear the deep tone of Robert's voice and the silvery laugh that greeted whatever remark he had made.

Sir Robert escorted Abigail back to the castle, trying to shorten his long strides as she seemed to dawdle along, clinging to his arm, talking about getting ready for the ball, sending for Matilda, dancing....he stopped listening, in a fever to leave her. At last she smiled sweetly at him and, with a final remark that she would see him in the hall later to help welcome their guests, she went indoors.

He quickened his pace again and headed for the stables. As he'd guessed, he found Martin leaning on the half door of the stall where the pony had spent the night. He looked up as Sir Robert came in.

"A nice little animal, brother. Matilda will be delighted. It is hard to believe she will be seven years of age tomorrow. I remember the day she was born."

Suddenly Sir Robert felt his jealousy and anger drain away and he leant on the door next to him. He was fond of Martin. He knew that although his brother had no head for business, preferred a life of idle enjoyment, he was nevertheless a good-hearted man. Could Catherine be seriously attracted? Surely if he himself loved her as much as he believed he did, he would only want what would make her happy? And if that was to marry Martin? He fought back the jealousy that threatened to rise again.

"As do I, of course. A lot has happened since then."

They stood in silence for a moment, remembering the good and the bad things that the Courtney family had experienced, then Sir Robert went on, "I understand only too well that your behaviour in a social sense is different from mine. But I need to know if your intentions towards Miss Collins are genuine or just an example of your usual flirtation."

Martin raised an eyebrow quizzically. "Miss Collins? Why, brother, she is a very fine girl, one whom, if my circumstances were better, I might well be inclined to pursue."

Sir Robert's hands tightened on the top of the half door and Martin glanced down in amusement at the white knuckles. It really was so easy to bait his brother, but perhaps not very sensible as he still hadn't agreed to pay off his latest gambling debts.

"And do you feel she has any feelings towards you?"

"Come, come, Robert. I would never dream of asking a young lady what she was feeling. Why do you need to know? Surely you are about to become engaged to Abigail, so the object of Catherine's affections is irrelevant?"

Sir Robert took a deep breath. "I need to know because I intend to ask Catherine Collins for permission to approach her father to ask for her hand in marriage."

For the first time in many years, Martin Courtney fell silent, unable to instantly reply. Eventually he said slowly, "And do you have reason to believe that Miss Collins returns your regard?"

A hot day, the stables, sunlight lancing through the windows, the smell of hay and horse and leather, bright brown hair cascading down over slim shoulders, his hand on her waist, the look in her eyes as he bent his head, meaning to kiss her... He loved her so much; could he possibly believe that his affections were returned? Surely she would not have looked at him with that expression in her eyes if she was indifferent.

"I hope so, yes. But I was concerned that you had...and if she preferred to be Mrs Martin Courtney, then..."

Martin smiled, held out his hand and Sir Robert grasped it. "I wish you joy, brother. Believe me, I have never had any doubts as to where Catherine's affections were directed and it certainly is not towards me. I also wish you success, although I fear you are about to set your feet on a path that is littered with obstacles."

They walked back towards the house in a companionable silence. Martin found himself envying Robert - he wondered if he would ever feel as strongly for a woman - so strongly that he was about to incur the wrath and disappointment of many people. He also found himself wondering if that strong streak of common-sense he knew existed in the fairy girl would raise its head and demand to be heard. To come from being the daughter of a country parson to being Lady Courtney, knowing you could bring nothing to the marriage but yourself, would she think that a step too far? If she cared deeply for Robert, would she risk hurting him in any way at all?

He gazed up at the sky as they reached the castle: ominous dark clouds were gathering out to sea. Hopefully the storm would not break until the next day, but break it would.

13

Six o'clock found Catherine sitting in front of her mirror, gazing at her reflection. She wasn't a girl who usually studied her own face - she would normally just check to make sure she had no smuts on her cheeks or that her hair wasn't escaping from its pins. But tonight she caught herself looking in detail at the rather plain girl whose big eyes appeared sad. She tried smiling at herself but that did nothing to cheer her up. She had to admit that compared to Abigail, she came a very poor second in looks. At least her hair was pretty: she had washed it and brushed it nearly dry.

A movement in the mirror caught her attention. Matilda was sitting on her bed, watching her, smiling.

"So, Miss Matilda, shall I dress my hair in a different style tonight? What do you think?" She looped up the long thick tresses and pinned them in loose ringlets above her ears. "Does this look less severe than my normal braids? I think so. Do you?"

In the mirror she could see the little girl nodding, then she jumped off the bed and coming over to Catherine, began to push under the pins, the heads of the flowers she had saved from those Mrs Crawford had used to decorate the dining-room.

Catherine laughed: she thought she looked like one of the fairies in Matilda's storybooks, but if it amused the little girl, she would let her continue. She could always take them out on her way downstairs.

Just as Matilda was finishing, a knock at the door brought in Abigail's maid. She raised her eyebrows at the flowers but just said, "My mistress is asking for Miss Matilda. She wishes to dress her for this evening."

Catherine swept her robe round her and stood up. "Of course. Listen, Matilda dear, you are to go to Miss Richmond's room. She has a lovely new dress for you to wear tonight. She will bring you downstairs and you will help your papa greet his guests. Now, be a very good girl and behave as nicely as I know you can."

Matilda thrust out her bottom lip and looked mutinous, but allowed herself to be taken out of the room. Catherine could hear the maid chivying her along the passage and hoped Abigail would not be too brisk with her.

A few minutes later another knock at the door brought in Bessie, leaning heavily on a cane, her ankle bandaged.

"Bessie! What are you doing out of bed and walking? You were told to rest."

"I thought I might be able to help in some little way. Getting ready for a grand dinner can be tiresome on your own."

"That is very kind of you. I must admit that the fastenings of my dress are difficult to manage."

Bessie glanced round. "Miss Matilda's gone to Miss Richmond, I take it?"

Catherine smiled; the way that the servants always knew everything that was happening in the castle without being told amused her. "Yes, there is a brand new dress waiting for her. Miss Richmond purchased it in Newcastle. I do hope Matilda likes it. It's very kind of Miss Richmond."

Bessie sniffed disdainfully and turned her attention to the dress lying across a chair. "Oh, that be a proper evening gown, Miss! I haven't seen it before."

Catherine picked up the creation and held it in front of her. It had been in one of Bennetta's parcels - the very latest fashion - dark gold, off the shoulder, with a great full skirt over several stiff petticoats. A wide border of lace ran from the front of the neck to the hem and big gold flowers had been sewn on every few inches.

"It was a gift from my cousin, Elizabeth Darcy, but I'm not sure I should wear it. It is so very formal, so low-cut and elaborate, highly fashionable. Perhaps it isn't right for me."

"Oh Miss, don't say that." Bessie was fingering the sumptuous material with glee. "Try it on. I reckon you'll be the grandest dressed lady at the party."

A few minutes later, Catherine stood, regarding her reflection. There was no doubt that the dress, stiff and fanciful, certainly altered her appearance. Gone was the governess, the poor relation to the Darcy family - a sophisticated, elegant woman was revealed, surely one Robert would not be able to trifle with. If he was going to dismiss her from the castle tomorrow, then she would go with her head held high.

The second she left her room, Catherine could hear the sound of many voices echoing up from the south hall. She peered over the banister to see that the main doors had been flung open and from outside she could hear the clatter of hooves, the rumble of carriage wheels and the cries from postillions and grooms.

Sir Robert, with Abigail at his side, were greeting the guests as they arrived. Maids were discreetly taking away cloaks and hats and there was much gaiety and laughter as footmen passed amongst the crowd with trays of refreshments. There was no sign of Matilda and Catherine wondered if perhaps the dress had not fitted.

As she watched Abigail being so charming, so elegant, her dress a sparkling blue and silver, sapphires at her neck and ears, welcoming the party goers as if this was her own home, a wave of depression and despair swept over Catherine. It was easy to be brave in the seclusion of your own room, but when you were faced with reality, it would be far easier to be a coward and retreat.

Suddenly she spotted Matilda. She was wandering through the hall, her fair hair cascading over her shoulders. The new dress was white and frilly with lots of lace and bows. It was a pretty garment, but Matilda did not look happy. Even as Catherine watched, she saw Robert turn from greeting the next arrival and glance round anxiously.

A look of annoyance flashed across Abigail's face, and she called out and beckoned to Matilda who hesitantly wandered across to stand between them. But even with her father's hand resting tenderly on her shoulder, she was refusing to look up and reply to the guests who bent to speak to her.

Making up her mind, Catherine sped along the corridor and down the spiral stairway. If she had just her own feelings to consider, then she would have retired back to her room but she could not bear to think of Matilda being unhappy.

She took the stairs at a more sedate pace than usual; drawing attention to herself by erupting into the gathering was something to be avoided this evening. Easing her way through the crowded hall, she stood a little way off from Sir Robert and Abigail as what seemed to be the last of their guests arrived and the main doors were shut.

"Oh, Miss Collins. There you are at last. Where have you been?" Abigail's voice was tight and angry. "We need you to take charge of Matilda. It is very remiss of you to be tardy in attending." She turned away before Catherine could reply.

Sir Robert gently pushed his daughter towards Catherine who took her hand in hers and gave it a comforting squeeze.

"I expect you have been busy getting ready, Miss Collins. You look very elegant. But perhaps you can take Matilda upstairs now and leave her in Bessie's care. I have shown her off to our friends and neighbours. There is no need for her to endure any more adult society tonight! I am afraid she has not enjoyed herself." His eyes darkened and he frowned. "Perhaps Abigail is right, perhaps a special school is what she needs."

Catherine glared at him - Matilda wasn't deaf, she would be upset by these remarks. "I'm afraid I do not agree, Sir. There is nothing wrong with Matilda except for her lack of speech. No school will make her talk. She will when she wants to and at the moment she doesn't want to!"

Sir Robert found his lips twitching; was this the famous "common-sense" that Elizabeth Darcy had told him about. It was like facing a tigress defending her cub.

"We will talk tomorrow, as I suggested. Now I must join my guests. I will see you at the dinner table, Miss Collins, but perhaps without - " He gestured towards her hair and, reaching forward, pulled out one or two fading flower heads, all that remained of Matilda's earlier decorations. Then under his breath he muttered, "I hardly recognised you in that fashionable dress, but the flowers in your hair told me that Miss Collins is still with us!"

"Sir - I must apologise - "

"I think we are about to go in for dinner. I should make haste, Catherine, or else your soup will be cold again. Matilda, my dear child, I will see you in the morning. Tomorrow is your birthday, don't forget! You will have reached the great age of seven! Go to sleep tonight wishing for what you want most in the world and your wishes might come true." He bent to kiss her and with a bow, returned to his guests.

Catherine hurried Matilda up the spiral stairway, aware that her cheeks were flaming and her heart pounding with every turn of the stairs. He hadn't recognised her in Bennetta's dress; what did that tell her? That he thought she was trying to ape Abigail, trying to be someone she wasn't?

With Matilda safe in Bessie's care, Catherine returned to her room and stared at her reflection. He was right. Oh, she looked well enough in gold silk, but the person she saw in the mirror wasn't her. It was someone pretending to be one of the Darcy girls - someone she would never be.

Swiftly, she pulled off the dress, uncaring that some of the hooks broke and threw the tightly fitting corset onto the floor. She would go down to dinner in one of her own gowns; it was a pale grey muslin with a dark green net overthrow gathered under the bosom. She needed no corset as the loose folds hung to her feet, comfortably and easily.

She shook out the silly ringlets over her ears and pulled her hair up carelessly into a loose knot on neck. Then she looked in the mirror again and saw Catherine Collins standing there; slim and old-fashioned, no doubt, but no imitation of anyone else.

By the time she had reached the south hall again it was empty and she could hear the buzz of laughter and talk coming from the dining-room. Footmen and maids were busy moving from the kitchens to serve the first course and Catherine hoped she could slip in unnoticed.

"Ha, Miss Collins. I see you too are late to the party." Lady Honoria appeared from the passageway that led to the north hall, leaning heavily on her walking stick. Tonight, she was wearing dark red, from her elaborate hair ornament to the tips of her velvet shoes. The rubies at her neck and on her fingers glowed in the candlelight.

"Lady Honoria," Catherine dropped a low curtsey, "Yes, I am afraid I am. I decided to change my dress. It was not....suitable for the company."

The bright beady eyes glanced at her with interest. "Hmmm, and I take it the child will not be eating with us."

Catherine offered the old lady her arm and they slowly moved towards the dining-room. "Indeed no. Sir Robert told her to go to bed and wish for what she wanted more than anything in the world. Did you know he is giving her a pony."

"And he thinks that is what she wishes for most? Ha! My nephew is a good man but sadly lacking in imagination."

Catherine had no reply. Perhaps Lady Honoria did not fully understand how much Matilda loved horses, how long she had wished for one of her own.

The footman flung the door open and the noise from forty people swept out and around them. Lady Honoria tapped Catherine on the arm with her fan and was then guided to her seat a few places away from Sir Robert and Abigail.

Catherine was not surprised to find that the only other empty chair was at the very far end of the table, hard against the wall but she was only too relieved to sit down and hoped her entrance had not been noticed. But when she raised her gaze, she found she was looking straight down the board at Sir Robert and even at that distance, she could see he was raising an eyebrow, obviously annoyed at her late arrival and her unassuming attire.

"Miss Collins - I did not see you come in. You have been putting young Matilda to bed, I suppose."

Martin was speaking, only three places down from her and across, raising his wine glass to her in welcome. "My friends, may I introduce Miss Catherine Collins, related to our new sister-in-law Cassandra and to the Darcys of Pemberley, whom you may have heard of. Miss Collins is spending a few months with us here and is devoted to my niece."

Catherine felt pleasure at his kind remarks. She had no desire to make more of herself than she was, but there was no denying that her links to the Darcys - something she could never have mentioned herself - broke the ice with her dinner companions.

Martin signaled for the footman to replenish his glass, sitting back in his chair and watching the guests, listening to the gossip and talk with little interest. He was certain he had heard thunder in the distance recently, a rumbling out to sea that foretold the coming storm. Even with the windows open the air was still and heavy, the flames from the candles in their old silver candelabra that he hadn't seen on the table for many a year, standing bright and yellow without a single flicker.

He wished the storm would break - the one outside and the one threatening his own family as well. He glanced down the length of the table - there was his brother, frowning as he swirled the wine round his glass, then bending his head to talk to the lady on his left, the wife of their nearest neighbours.

Abigail was seated on his right but Martin could tell from her expression that the evening was not going in the way she had planned. That was not the face of a young woman who had just received the proposal of marriage she had been waiting for so anxiously. She was speaking to no one beyond curt replies to any questions she was asked.

He looked to his left and found himself smiling - his fairy girl, wearing an old-fashioned gown and no ornaments in her hair, had obviously conquered her dinner companions. She was listening intently to a verbose elderly gentleman on her left, then turning to bring the nervous looking woman on her right into the conversation. Surely Robert had yet to speak to her about marriage? She seemed unflustered, even a little sad, not the face of a young woman who could shortly become Lady Courtney.

The meal continued on, course after course, the voices got louder, the laughter more shrill; then, just after the arrival of platters of cheese and silver bowls laden with fruit, both candied and fresh, a sudden gust of wind blew through the windows, sending the candles dancing. A new sound came above the notes of the musicians outside, the soft patter of rain followed by a rumble of thunder. At last, the weather had broken and the poor men outside would be soaked unless someone gave them permission to abandon their posts.

Catherine glanced down the table; as hostess it was Abigail's duty to cope with such a problem, but she was engrossed in leaning on Sir Robert's shoulder, laughing at some remark he had made, insisting that his portion of strawberries was too small. Catherine's gaze met Sir Robert's and even in the candlelight she could see the blue blaze that made her tremble. He nodded towards the windows and she gestured to a footman and whispered that the musicians should come indoors now and get ready for the dancing in the ballroom.

"Ha! Nicely done, girl." Lady Honoria was leaning forward and tapped her spoon several times against her fruit bowl. "Robert!" Her voice wasn't that loud but sharp and imperious. "Miss Collins has ordered the musicians indoors. And quite rightly. So I think it time we all moved into the ballroom. Coffee can be served in there and I would like another ice and to see some dancing before I retire for the evening."

In the confusion of everyone moving through the south hall into the ballroom, Catherine managed to slip unnoticed up the spiral stairway and along to the night nursery. The storm was easing, the rain now just drizzle; a strong wind had cleared the air. She wanted to make certain that Matilda hadn't been too worried by the thunder.

To her surprise she found the child sitting by the open window in her nightgown, gazing out at the rough sea where huge white horses were flying across from the horizon. The wind was blowing hard, sending the storm inland and a full moon now sailed across the sky between the ragged remnants of the clouds, illuminating the crashing waves and flying spray as it hit the beach below the Courtney peninsula.

Matilda looked round and smiled; clearly, she wasn't the slightest bit worried by the view. Bessie was nowhere to be seen; there was just Peggy, the youngest housemaid, tidying up toys and folding clothes.

"Oh Miss Collins, I'm right glad you're here. I can't make the little miss go to bed. She wants to look at the sea."

"Where's Bessie?"

"Her foot was powerful bad again tonight. She shouldn't have walked on it earlier. Mrs Crawford said she must rest it at once and asked me to look after Miss Matilda until you came upstairs."

Catherine put her arm round Matilda's shoulders and ushered her into bed. "You must go to sleep now, dear child, because tomorrow is your birthday and you must be bright and happy and up early. And don't forget to wish for what you want most - wishes on your birthday can come true, you know!" She smiled as she pulled the bed-covers over her shoulders, remembering the little pony out in the stables.

Matilda reached out sleepily and pulled her mother's miniature closer so she could see it. Catherine's eyes filled with tears; she did hope that the little girl had not over-heard Abigail talking about sending her away to school. She would be so frightened to go far from home. Surely Sir Robert would not allow it?

Catherine made up her mind; she had already decided not to attend the rest of the evening, she wouldn't be missed and it would give her no pleasure to watch Robert and Abigail dancing together. But Matilda's future was more important than her own feelings. Catherine needed to speak to him tonight about that; whatever he wanted to say to her about her own future here at Courtney, even if he wanted to apologise for his behaviour earlier, that could wait for another day. She needed to hear him promise Matilda would not be sent away, then she could tell the child this evening, if she were still awake, or at least first thing in the morning.

"Peggy, stay here with her, please. I shall not be long."

"But Mrs Crawford said I had to go back to the kitchens as soon as you came up, Miss." The young girl looked anxious; obviously incurring the wrath of Mrs Crawford on this important occasion was not something she wished to do.

"I will be very quick."

Taking the spiral staircase at top speed, Catherine was glad to find the south hall empty except for a couple of footmen. From the ballroom came loud music and a great chatter of people. She slipped through the door, the heat and noise swirling round her in a cloud. The powder sprinkled on the wooden floor was being raised by dancing feet and hung in the air like a fine mist. The bright colours of dresses, the glitter of jewels, the screech of a violin out of tune, all made her head swim.

A dance had just finished and the musicians were beginning to play the introduction for the next one. She gazed urgently round the room, where was Sir Robert?

"Why, Catherine, isn't this the dance you promised me?"

It was Martin, standing, smiling at her, holding out his hand.

"Oh forgive, me, Martin, but I have to find - "

"Miss Collins." The voice that she would recognise through any crowd, through any thunder storm, made her twist round. Sir Robert took her hand and, with a bow to his surprised brother, lead her out onto the dance floor.

14

The tune being played was slow and stately, more suitable for the older members of the party. Catherine felt relieved; she knew these steps well which was all to the good because her mind was too full to think of which foot went in front of which. She was, however, aware that a lot of people were looking at them and, as she turned once round, she couldn't help but see Abigail standing next to Martin, glowering across the room at her.

"I thought you had decided to abandon us for the rest of the evening." The strong warm hand holding hers tightened as they progressed down the room, slowly, in step.

"I needed to check that Matilda had not been upset by the thunder."

"I could have told you she would be perfectly happy. She has very little fear of nature in any of its guises. She is - " there was a pause, then, " - she is very like her mother in that respect."

"Hopefully she will grow up, afraid of nothing and no one. But, Sir Robert, I was hoping to talk to you about that very thing - Matilda growing up."

At that moment she swung away and round the next man in line before linking hands with Robert again who bent his head to murmur, "Catherine - there are things I have to say to you. Things I must say. I meant to leave it until tomorrow, but when I see you, I can't help myself. I need to talk tonight."

The music swung them apart again and Catherine took the opportunity to stiffen her resolve not to get upset. If he was about to ask her to leave Courtney, then she would quietly agree, only beg him not to send Matilda away to school.

His hand was on hers again and she dared a brief sideways glance to find that dark blue gaze fixed on her face and the expression brought hot colour flooding up into her cheeks.

Suddenly he muttered something violently under his breath. "This is idiocy! I have guests I cannot ignore. Miss Collins - Catherine - ices are being served, I believe. Will you wait for me in the drawing-room, please? I will bring you one there."

"Yes, thank you. There is something I have to say to you, too. Something very important."

He squeezed her hand, almost painfully crushing her fingers and they danced on in silence - she was aware of a dreadful passion in his expression, but whether it was anger or dislike or - but she refused to let herself speculate any further.

Eventually the music came to a close and clapping, they bowed and curtseyed to each other and parted - Sir Robert was immediately hailed by some of his guests and Catherine moved swiftly through the crowd, keeping her head down, determined to avoid Martin and Abigail. The drawing-room was deserted, thank goodness. Most of the candles had been snuffed out and only two on the mantelpiece glimmered in gloom. But the drapes had not been pulled across and brilliant moonlight flooded into the room. From the shore, Catherine could hear the thudding of the surf on the beach, like a distant drum, hastening her to her fate.

She flung open the little mullioned window, letting the cold breeze cool her cheeks. She stared up at the moon, so pale and far away.

"Catherine!"

She spun round: Robert was closing the door behind him, placing a bowl of iced rose water on a table and crossing to her. He took both her hands in his and chafed them. "You're cold. Let me shut this window."

"No, please. I love the fresh sea air, especially after a storm. I am not cold." She tried to pull her hands away, but his grip tightened and bravely she raised her head to meet his gaze.

"Catherine, first of all, I must apologise for my behaviour yesterday in the stables. To treat you, a guest in my home, in such a cavalier fashion, I am deeply ashamed of myself. In my defence, you looked so charming, so beautiful, so desirable - but for all of that, I was still at fault, and I would ask your forgiveness."

"Of course, Sir. I think the extreme heat can cause people to behave in strange ways. I have not given it another thought and beg you to do the same."

Sir Robert frowned and tightened his grasp, sliding his fingers up her wrists on to the bare skin under her sleeves. "But I can't forget. Catherine, please do me the honour of accepting my proposal of marriage. I want you so very much to be my wife."

For a few long seconds, Catherine felt her world spin in a joy of colour and excitement. Robert wanted her to marry him. This man she loved so dearly wanted her to be his wife, to care for him and his daughter, to help him with the Courtney estates. And just as that thought crossed her mind, the spinning world jolted to an unhappy stop and reality came crashing in.

Robert had proposed marriage, but didn't love her, those words had never been spoken - he desired her. She was wise enough in the ways of the world to know that there was a great difference between the two emotions. And even if she put all that to one side and followed her own heart, she was only too aware that she could bring nothing to such an alliance. Her papa would be hard pressed to find even a hundred guineas as a dowry; she could offer no money to help with the estate, no connections that would help Robert in the years ahead. She had a vague connection to the Darcys of Pemberley, of course, but Richard, his own brother, was already linked to them in a far closer connection than hers.

She gazed up into the stern face that she loved so much; the moon was behind a cloud now and she could not see his expression. What could she say? How could she reject him without causing great offence?

"Sir, you are too nice. We were both overwhelmed by proximity and the heat of the day. Your apology is quite enough for me. There is no need for you to change all your plans on a whim."

"A whim?" His warm grasp fell away from her skin, leaving it chilled. "You think I propose marriage, to make you my wife, to make you Lady Courtney, on a whim?"

Catherine took a deep breath and said quietly. "I think that perhaps you have taken events out of proportion. Of course, I am deeply honoured by the esteem you show me of asking me to be your wife, but, of course I am sure you will be relieved when I say I must decline."

The moon sailed into view again and the room was bathed in silver light. Sir Robert stared down at the slim figure in front of him. He didn't know whether he was angry or dismayed. He had been so certain that Catherine returned his feelings. Sometimes he had caught her looking at him and the expression on her face - surely he couldn't have been so wrong. A flicker of temper, of passion that had been shut away for so many years, never ignited, never explored, began to flare.

"Perhaps, if it does not inconvenience you in any fashion, Miss Collins, you could inform me exactly why you decline my proposal."

Catherine was stung by the change in his tone. Now there was anger; rejection, even if it was secretly welcomed, was bound to annoy any gentleman.

"Sir, I am well aware that your engagement to Miss Richmond has been expected at any time. I have no doubt of where your true feelings lie. You feel that your behaviour in the stables yesterday put you into debt to me, perhaps you think my reputation has been sullied in some way. You are being a perfect gentleman in your actions, but there is no need."

"And that is what you truly believe? That I am trying to make amends for a moment's aberration?"

"Sir, what else would you have me believe? I have no money to bring to Courtney Castle, no connections to offer."

"You think money comes into this?" His voice had changed, become harsh. "Catherine, do you really think so poorly of me that you believe I would marry just for money?"

Catherine felt tears begin to sting her eyes. She just wanted this dreadful conversation to be over, to run away and hide somewhere, anywhere, of his sight.

"I have been told you are in dire need of capital for the estate, Sir," she whispered. "But I think you would only marry if affection were there, too. All I beg of you is that when you and Miss Richmond are wed, you change your mind and do not send Matilda away from Courtney to some special school. I truly believe that is the worst thing that could happen to her."

Sir Robert took a step back into the dark gloom of the drawing-room. Her words cut him to the very heart, partly, of course, because there was a sliver of truth in them. For many months he had thought of marrying Abigail and he wouldn't have been human if he hadn't realised that the money she would bring would be useful.

In his defence, it hadn't just been the money that motivated him, he had been fond of her for years: it had seemed an eminently suitable match, one all his family had thought right, but he had never loved her. If he had never gone to Pemberley, never seen this slight figure dancing barefoot on the grass, her bright brown hair flying in the wind.... he had never thought he could fall in love so painfully and now so hopelessly.

He glanced up at the portrait of Lucinda, as much a mystery to him now in death as she had been when she was alive. What he had felt for her had been a young man's longing to possess something beautiful and strange. This overwhelming love and passion he felt for Catherine was like comparing a candle to a raging fire.

"I am sorry you think so badly of me, Miss Collins, that you think I would do anything to distress my daughter, whom I love dearly. You must consider me a poor type of man indeed."

"No, Sir – " Catherine interrupted him, " - I know you care for her, but I truly believe - "

"Let us talk no more." He took another step back from her and she could no longer see his expression. "Your opinion of my character will obviously prevent you from looking on my proposal with favour. I can only apologise for misreading your feelings towards me and for taking up your valuable time this evening. And now I must return to my guests and I am sure you would wish to continue with your dancing. My brother is probably waiting anxiously for you to make an appearance. Perhaps his character is more to your liking!"

The last words were spoken heatedly, angrily, a man who had just had all his hopes turn to dust and he turned on his heel and walked swiftly out of the room. Having gained the hall, he plunged his hand into his breast pocket and pulled out the scarlet ribbon he kept next to his heart. For a second, he stared at it and was about to throw it to the ground - but then he stopped. It was all he had of the girl he loved; he would not discard it in temper.

A footman passing into the ballroom with a tray of wine glasses let out the noise of laughter and music. Sir Robert took a deep breath; he had guests to entertain. No one must ever know what had just occurred. He didn't understand how he could have misread the situation so badly and wondered how he could ever bear to face Catherine Collins again.

Catherine couldn't remember ever feeling such pain before. She had heard of people being broken-hearted, but had never truly believed it possible. But now she knew better - her heart was in pieces, she had turned down marriage to the man she loved and had managed to do it clumsily, stupidly, in a way that had made him believe she thought only the worst of him.

She wanted to run after Robert, tell him that she knew he was an honourable man, that she was thinking only of him and his life here at Courtney Castle. She wanted him to hold her hands again, warm and safe in his grasp, and tell him she loved him and always would. But she could do none of these things.

The thought of returning to the ballroom was abhorrent - surely one glance at her face would tell Abigail and even Martin, that some traumatic event had occurred.

Waiting until the south hall was momentarily empty of footmen and maids, Catherine slipped out of the main door and hurried through the moonlit night into the quiet sanctuary of the walled garden. She crept into the shadow of a pergola covered with white roses and sank down onto the seat. Only then would she allow the tears to come, in great gasps that shook her body.

She had no idea how long she sat crouched there, her head buried in her arms but eventually she realised she was very cold, she had run out without a cloak and the grey and green evening dress was damp with both tears and dew.

. . .

With a shudder, she sat up, hugging her knees to her chest. Her eyes were dry now; she doubted if she had any tears left to shed. She knew it must by now be the early hours of the morning. Faintly, towards the horizon with the sea she could see that the sky was a paler shade of dark blue, dawn was on its way.

Wearily Catherine made her way back to the castle; she knew the little side door into the sculleries would be open; even at this hour, servants would be up and about their work, cleaning up after the party, tidying and polishing, preparing breakfast.

The upper floors were silent, everyone sound asleep. Her room had never looked so inviting, all she wanted to do was sink onto the bed and sleep, waking to the realisation that this night had just been some dreadful dream and not the horrible reality that she knew it to be.

She pulled off the evening dress and found one of her old warm day dresses that she had packed away in a trunk - plain, brown and unfashionable - the dress of common-sense, the dress of a parson's daughter who had turned down the chance to become Lady Courtney. She wanted to start packing because now it was impossible that she could remain here at the castle, facing Robert across the breakfast table, making polite conversation in the evenings, discussing Matilda -

Matilda! Oh, how could she leave before a replacement had been found to care for Matilda? And today was the child's seventh birthday, she would be given the pony and expect that Catherine would be there to go riding with her.

The sky to the east on the far horizon was growing paler - dawn was here and the sun would be rising on a new day, one Catherine had no idea how she was going to survive. She pulled on her stoutest boots - she would walk through the gardens and out onto the moorland before Matilda woke and try to calm herself. She would call on the common-sense that everyone said she had and force herself to face a future without love, because there would be no way she could possibly marry another man feeling the way she did about Sir Robert Courtney.

The castle was beginning to stir. Two young housemaids were already busy sweeping and dusting the south hall as Catherine made her way out into the cool dawn air. She could hear laughter from the kitchen area and wondered if she would ever be able to smile and laugh again. Could you stay sad all your life? Perhaps with a broken heart that would not be difficult.

She wandered out through the gardens where she had hidden through those painful hours, on past the paddocks, where one of the grooms wished her a good morning and up a grassy track that led to the top of a hill.

The wind was stronger up here and she bravely turned to face it, glad of the cold sting that dried the tears on her cheeks. She could see for miles, out to where the sea met the sky. The storm had passed, but it looked as if another one was brewing on the horizon which was dark with clouds. The waves were racing towards the shore, driven by the wind, white horses of spray blowing before them.

How she loved this part of the world! She stared down at Courtney Castle. The red and black flag was flying bravely from one of the turrets and she could see tiny figures in the stable yard.

From on high she realised just how large the castle was; she was certain there were rooms she had never entered, floors she had never explored. She would have been more than happy to have lived here for the rest of her life, but she knew she had to return to Pemberley at least, and then on to wherever Elizabeth Darcy could find her a good position.

She would hear about Robert and Martin through their brother, no doubt. Learn of Robert's marriage and discover what happened to Matilda. She would hopefully discover how to treat this episode in her life as some wonderful dream, a time apart from reality, a few weeks she could look back on with tenderness, not this current haze of pain.

"Catherine!"

She turned, startled, as she heard her name being called from further down the slope. It was Sir Robert, bare headed, his coat flying open, his long legs eating up the path towards her. Oh, this was too much! To follow her when it was obvious she desired seclusion. Surely, he had no need to chastise her further, to continue their conversation.

She hurried down the path towards him, her feet slipping a little on the damp moss and he reached out a hand to stop her precipitous descent before hastily letting her arm loose again. "Catherine - Miss Collins - " Sir Robert looked past her, his face stern. "Matilda? She is not with you? I thought you had taken her out early as some sort of birthday treat?"

"Matilda? Sir, she will still be asleep at this hour. Surely, she will be in her room." Catherine suddenly felt very cold and pushed back her long brown hair from her face, realising how wild she must look without a bonnet or hair pins.f

Sir Robert stared down at her. "Her room is empty! I couldn't sleep - " He paused, embarrassed, and Catherine felt the hot colour flood into her own face. "I thought to be with her when she woke on her birthday, but her bed is cold and the little maid was fast asleep on her pallet and didn't know where the child could be. I naturally thought she was with you. But if you haven't seen her - then where can she be? Oh my God, Catherine. What has happened to her?"

15

Distressed, Catherine swayed and without thinking, reached for his hand. The strength and warm of his grip helped her to pull herself together. She forced herself to think logically. There was probably a very simple explanation and she gasped it out as they hurried back down the path towards the castle.

“Bessie Stokes! She may have gone to see Bessie, upstairs in the servants’ quarters. She might think, child-like, that her maid would have a gift for her on her birthday.”

“That occurred to me, too. I sent a footman to her room; Bessie has not seen her, and when I found your room empty, I was certain you had both gone out. The maid tells me her cloak and boots are missing. Catherine - if anything should happen to her - ”

She winced at the pain in his voice as the grip on her fingers tightened and fought to reassure him. “Nothing will have happened to her, Robert. She is a bright, intelligent child, completely at home in the castle. There will be a sensible explanation for her disappearance. Why, she may have already been found. We will check the stables straight away. That is my first thought.”

But when they reached the yard, they found Martin already there, having been woken by a tearful Mrs Crawford who by now had servants searching all over the castle. Martin's face went very still when he realised his brother and Catherine were alone.

"So, she was not with you! I was certain that would be the case. Robert, I have searched the stables and the grooms have been up in the haylofts in case she fell or was trapped in some way and could not shout out, of course. But there is no sign of her, and no one has seen her this morning."

Sir Robert realised he was still holding Catherine's hand and let it go reluctantly. "It is an old building. There are all sorts of little passages and stairways, especially in the upper floors."

"Mrs Crawford is searching them all. Our aunt wishes to be informed immediately we find Matilda, and Abigail has sent her maid to inquire."

"But she has not chosen to search herself!" Sir Robert's voice was harsh and Catherine felt a thrill of shame because she realised he was deeply disappointed in Miss Richmond's behaviour.

Suddenly Bessie appeared in the yard, hobbling towards them, her ginger hair uncovered, her apron obviously yesterday's. The freckles on her face stood out in stark relief against the pallor of her skin.

"Oh Miss Collins, Maister, where can she be? That stupid Peggy! I should have been there in her room. I would have heard her leave and stopped her."

Catherine could find no words to comfort her, then she had a thought. "I am told her heavy shoes are missing and her cloak. So, this is not some childish prank where she is playing hide and seek from us. She has gone out, warmly dressed, and the boots mean - "

"The beach!" Sir Robert said hoarsely. "She has gone to the shore - or perhaps to watch the fishing boats come into harbour at dawn with their nightly catch. Lucinda used to take her when she was no more than a baby. She enjoys that, but she knows she must never go by herself."

"The shore will be a dreadful rough place this morning," Bessie cried. "The storm last night has stirred up the sea wicked. And there is something else missing. I looked in her room - the miniature of her mama. It is always by her bedside and it isn't there this morning. Peggy swears it was there last night. She said Miss Matilda asked to hold it before she fell asleep."

"But why would she have taken that with her?" Sir Robert sounded confused, desperate. "Why would she leave the castle on her birthday? I told her last night that her dearest wish might come true today. She is getting the pony she wanted so much. Why would she wander off?"

Catherine felt as if someone had poured a great ewer of cold water down her back as she began to see what they were all missing. She could never say that she knew Matilda better than her father, but she did know a lot about little girls and the way their minds worked. "I told her the same thing, but we are both wrong - her greatest wish isn't for a pony," she said quietly, "It is to see her mother again."

There was a silence, then Sir Robert reached out a hand again and Catherine clasped it in hers, all thoughts of their estrangement put aside.

"But she knows her mother is dead!" he said.

"She was just five years of age when the accident happened. Perhaps she has never fully understood that Lady Courtney is never coming back. She has been unable to talk about it. I imagine she did not attend the funeral and you have never mentioned the accident for fear of upsetting her."

Sir Robert nodded. "My aunt wanted her to go to the church but I said no and I gave strict orders that no one should mention it in front of her. But we do talk about Lucinda, we try to keep her memories of her mother alive, that is only right."

"So perhaps in her child-like mind, she believes her mama has just gone away and will come back one day, especially if she wishes for it on her birthday!"

"And my granma was talking to her about wishes when we visited the other day. You remember, Miss Collins, the little maid loves those stories."

A memory stirred in Catherine's mind. "There was a special one she liked hearing from you, about three wishes and an emerald cave."

Bessie looked unhappy. "That's just an old fairy story, Miss. No one believes it."

Catherine and Sir Robert gazed at each other, realisation dawning. "No adult believes it," she said, "but a seven year old girl, one who has listened to those stories all her life, who has been told that if she wishes for what her heart desires, she will get it? I can see that might well think it true."

Sir Robert's grasp on her hand tightened until she could have winced with the pain. "It makes sense, Catherine. The poor child has gone find an emerald cave to wish for Lucinda to come back."

Catherine shuddered. "And I know where she will look. The caves we saw when we went to the fishing village to visit old Mrs Stokes. Bessie, you told me they are not difficult to reach once the tide is out."

"It was out an hour or more ago," Bessie said. "Walking along the shoreline would be easy, Sir."

"And soon it will turn and come racing in! And after that storm, it will be a high tide, any cave will be flooded."

"She cannot have got far. She wouldn't have set out in the dark." Catherine was trying to be calm. "If we hurry, we will probably see her along the beach and can call to her."

Sir Robert took a deep breath. "Thank God for your cool head, Catherine. You are quite right. She is a brave, intelligent little thing. She will not put herself into danger out of stupidity. Come, we must hurry."

Afterwards, Catherine could remember little of them leaving the castle. She had a vague memory of Sir Robert shouting instructions at various servants, ordering a weeping Mrs Crawford to inform his aunt of what was happening and to bring blankets and hot drinks down to the shore as soon as possible.

He begged Martin to search the gardens and grounds again, in case they were wrong in their assumptions and then to ride to the fishing village. He was sure that if they were used for hiding smuggled goods, as he had often suspected, the fishermen would be reluctant in ordinary circumstances to tell anyone in authority how to access the caves from the land, but he was certain when they realised a child was in danger they would agree to help.

Then Catherine was following him out onto the peninsula, down the steps onto the beach, the sand firm under her feet, the sun beginning to inch up into the heavens, showing a tangled mass of seaweed, torn fishing nets, broken pieces of wood and other debris thrown up by the high tide during the storm. The sea was still rough, big white topped waves were crashing onto the shore, the foam hissing on the sand like a thousand snakes.

"Catherine - look, footprints. Small boots. They must be from Matilda!"

"We were right. She has come this way."

"Hurry. The tide is turning."

"Go on ahead. You move faster than me."

He hesitated, then spun round to her. "Take care, my Catherine. I know you do not care for me, but I couldn't live if I were to lose both of you today." He touched his lips to her fingers and before she could reply, he was away, running along the shoreline, heading for the rocky barrier that shut off the cliff face where the caves were to be found.

'Oh my love, I do care for you. Most deeply and profoundly,' she thought and sent all her prayers winging after him.

Sir Robert was out of sight by the time Catherine reached the spit of great black boulders that stretched out into the sea, making a natural breakwater, shutting off one little cove from the next. She gazed doubtfully at the rocks - the tide was already coming in, the little stretch of sand at the far end of the rocks was already under water. There was no way she could walk around, as Matilda had probably done; she would have to climb up and over the obstacle.

She flung her thick shawl down on top of the razor sharp edges and hoisted herself up, scrambling down the other side, wincing a little as her ankles jarred on rounded pebbles that were already under water that swirled and sucked at the hem of her dress, soaking her stockings up to her knees. The waves were racing in faster and faster now, driven by another storm that was beginning to form somewhere over the horizon.

In the face of the cliff ahead of her, Catherine could see the opening of a cave, a black hole, low down on the rock face and realised the water would soon rush in, impossible to stop. She struggled to the entrance. "Robert! Matilda! Robert! Are you there?"

"Catherine! I've found her. But don't come in. It is too dangerous. Get help."

She gasped as a strong wave battered at her legs and she staggered to keep her balance.

"Catherine!" She turned as she heard her voice carried towards her from afar on the strong wind. Martin, together with a group of fishermen from the village, were hurrying towards her. She hesitated, but they were still some way off. She knew that the common-sense thing to do was wait until they reached her, but this was no time for common-sense, for following her head. Her heart insisted on action, insisted that she be at Robert's side, no matter what the outcome.

Bending double, Catherine waded inside the cave; luckily it was higher inside and she could stand up straight. The sides of the cave were dark and dripping - high above a crack in the rock face let in a beam of light, just enough to banish the dark a little. Now up to his waist in water, Sir Robert was gazing up to where a narrow ledge ran the length of the cave. Somehow Matilda had managed to scramble up a pile of loose rocks, but had obviously dislodged them as she did so. Catherine could see her small, frightened face staring down at them.

"Catherine! Oh my dear girl, why have you put yourself in danger?"

"I belong at your side," she replied, not caring if she was being forward or not, not caring if he thought the less of her for her remark.

A flash of pure happiness crossed his face but then vanished as the child struggled towards them. "Don't move, Matilda! We will come up to you." Sir Robert turned to Catherine. "If I lift you, I think you should be able to reach the ledge. Will you try?"

"But what about you?" Catherine smeared back long tendrils of hair that were splattered across her face.

"The water is going to rise in here quickly. Lord - the entrance is already impassable! Look at the speed the tide is making. I can keep myself afloat until I can reach the ledge but I fear for your safety. Come, Catherine, do you trust me?"

"Always," she replied gravely and was briefly aware of the gleam in his eyes as she turned so he could put both hands round her waist and, lifting her, threw her up onto the ledge.

For a long few seconds, she lay half onto the slippery stone and half with her legs and feet trying to gain a purchase. Then her boots found the wall and she pushed herself higher. Gasping, she edged her way along to Matilda and pulled the child into her arms. "We are here. Your papa is here. You are safe now, darling girl."

Matilda clung to her for a few moments and then turned to peer back over the edge. In the seconds since Catherine had left his arms, Robert was already up to his chest in foaming, angry water. He had cast off his coat that had been weighing him down, but even as he trod water, reaching for the ledge, a violent swell filled the cave, pulling him under.

"Papa!!!" The cry rang out, high and squeaky, from a throat that had not made many sounds for two years.

"Robert!" The anguish in Catherine's voice was what Sir Robert heard as he fought his way to the surface, shaking water from his face, reaching out as the water swirled round him. With a powerful surge, his hands clasped the ledge, he heaved himself up and, soaking wet with water running from his hair and shirt, wrapped his arms round both of them.

"Thank God you are both safe! Matilda - oh my dear child. You are so cold. Catherine - "

"Robert - Robert - listen, she spoke. Matilda spoke!"

Loosening his grip a little, he stared down at the face turned up to his, sea water dripping off his hair and running down his face. "Catherine - what do you mean?"

"She called out 'Papa' when you vanished under the water! Matilda, tell your papa you love him."

The little girl, held close, sheltered between the two of them, lifted her arms and wrapped them round her father's neck. "Love you, Papa!"

Suddenly Sir Robert's face was wet with more than sea water. He pulled them both close, wrapping his arms as tightly round them as he could, giving silent thanks for this miracle.

It was hard to tell how long they sat there, cold and wet on the narrow ledge, but at last Sir Robert said, "Catherine, dear heart, I know you refused my hand in marriage before, but I have to ask you again. I know this is not the time or place, but I fear I did not make it plain to you how much I love you, and I am determined you must know that, whatever happens to us in this dreadful place. You will say that you can bring nothing into our union, but you are wrong. You bring your sweet self and that is all I want, all I need. What does Martin call you, a fairy girl? Well, you have come into our lives here at Courtney and enchanted us all. You have won my heart and if you leave now, it will be broken for ever."

A bubble of laughter began to form inside Catherine and she felt it rising up until she was smiling, her eyes bright with happiness. "Well, Sir Robert - "

"Robert, please!"

"Well, Robert...as my reputation will now be in tatters, because until the tide turns again, I will be alone with you - except for dear Matilda, who can't really act as a chaperone - then I fear I must put aside my scruples and say yes to your proposal."

He glanced down at her anxiously, then smiled, too, when he saw she was joking, that the love shining from her eyes was all he would ever want.

"So, Miss Matilda, how will you like having Miss Collins as your new mama?" The dark wet head bent lovingly towards the fair one nestled on his shoulder.

"Mama Cathy," came the unexpected reply and Catherine felt a surge of joy. To win Robert's love was one thing, but to have Matilda as her daughter was a double blessing.

"Look, Catherine, it might be wet and bedraggled, but it has never left its place next to my heart."

She glanced up and smiled in surprised delight. From his shirt pocket Robert had taken a very wet, very grubby red ribbon - the same one that had once adorned her summer straw hat. And she knew that if they ever got back to the castle, she would show him the silly little button off his shirt that she kept safely in her sewing box and knew he would understand perfectly.

"I think I must be dreaming," she whispered a few minutes later. "I can hear voices. Are we dying, Robert? Have angels come to take us to heaven?" She shivered; she was so cold.

Sir Robert grinned and carefully loosened his grip on the two he loved most in life. "I think my brother has been called many things in his life, Catherine, but never an angel! Look, at the far end of the ledge, that is the light from a lantern coming towards us. I think this is one of the caves the local smugglers use - the ledge will, I believe, lead to a passageway that travels underground and comes out somewhere in the village. I have no doubt close by to where old Mrs Stokes lives! Help is on its way, dear heart. Hold close to me. All will be well."

Within minutes his prediction was confirmed. Martin had soon realised the tide prevented a rescue from the sea and together with the fishermen, including Bessie's father, had hurried back inland to the secret entrance which indeed was close to the Stokes' cottage.

Soon strong arms were helping them along the ledge and they were guided away from the sea, back down a dark, narrow rocky passageway towards the safety of the village.

As she reached the opening that led from the cave, Catherine turned and took one more look at the place where such terror and such happiness had visited her together. In the light from the mens' lanterns, she could see that bright green weeds hung in waving fronds from every wall - this indeed was old Mrs Stokes' "emerald cave", the place where wishes were granted.

16

"Dear Mama, I pray you and Papa and Harriet are all well and enjoying the summer in Hertfordshire. I expect Papa has been busy in the garden and I trust his vegetables have flourished this year. I long to hear all your news; Harriet must be growing tall by now.

"You will no doubt have been wondering what I shall be doing when I leave Courtney Castle - you made it clear in your last letter that you thought I should look for another position as governess. At the time I agreed with what you said and decided to apply to Cousin Elizabeth for another recommendation. But events have conspired against me. I hope you will be pleased to learn

-

"Catherine?" A warm hand on her shoulder and she raised her head to find Robert standing there. She wondered why she had ever thought his face stern and unapproachable. He was all warmth and tender love and she was counting the weeks until she could be his wife.

"You have written to my papa, I believe. I thought this letter to my stepmother could go with yours in the packet."

The dark blue eyes looked concerned. "I still feel I should travel south to ask for your hand in marriage in person, but it is such a long way and

I know that by the time we reach Pemberley, we will have journeyed far enough."

Catherine smiled, unaware of the ink blot on her cheek, of the bright brown strands of hair escaping their pins. "Pemberley! Oh it will be lovely to see it again. I do so hope Cousin Elizabeth will be pleased and grant us our wish to marry there."

"I think everyone will rejoice that there is to be a new Lady Courtney and such a beautiful one. I am sure there will be no problem with you staying at Pemberley until the day itself, which I pray will not be long in coming. I shall lodge with Richard and Cassandra: I am writing to him at this very moment, so I must return to a letter that is a joy to compose. Your presence next door distracted me, sweetheart!" and Sir Robert bent to kiss his bride to be.

Catherine continued with her letter:

".....that I have accepted a proposal of marriage from Sir Robert Courtney. His letter to my father asking permission is enclosed with this missive. I have assured him that Papa will find no objection to the match. We have asked Cousin Elizabeth if she will kindly host our wedding at Pemberley, as it is halfway between our two families and thus convenient for all regarding travel.

"Sir Robert sends you his warmest regards and wishes me to tell you that he will cover all the expenses of the wedding and only trusts that my dear papa will be well enough to undertake the ceremony himself. I myself wish for nothing more, only for you to be pleased for me. I am sure you can imagine how happy I am."

Pushing the letter to one side, Catherine rose and went to the window of the little room next to Robert's study that he had insisted she used as her own private sitting-room. After their marriage it would be decorated exactly as she wished, but for now a pretty writing desk and elegant chair that had belonged to the last Lady Courtney had been discovered in the attics and brought downstairs, together with the vast tapestries that were to be cleaned and hung in the dining-room.

A bowl of roses on the desk filled the room with their scent. She pushed open the window and leaned out; she could see the cobbled yard that led to the stables. Shouts of laughter rang out and a fat little fell pony came into view, led by Martin, with Matilda in the saddle, her bonnet flying.

"Not too fast, my dear. Be careful, Martin."

"Mama Cathy, Mama Cathy, watch me ride!" The child was talking more and more each day, a miracle that no one could explain except that the fear of losing her father had somehow released her from her affliction.

Martin Courtney waved his hat towards his soon to be sister-in-law. Everything was turning out exactly as he had hoped. Robert was in such a good mood that he had handed over the necessary funds without a word of reproach and Martin was relieved to think of all the future little Courtneys that would stand happily between him and the title. He just hoped they would not be too long in beginning that project!

He was sorry for Abigail but this rural life in the wilds of Northumberland would never have suited her. Angry and confused, she had headed for London as soon as Robert and Catherine had made their announcement and he intended to visit her there when he got a chance. He was quite certain he would find her surrounded by rich young men but whether any of them would want to offer for her hand was another thing altogether.

Catherine had returned to her letters.

"My dear Bennetta, I hope this letter finds you well and not too unhappy amongst the hills and heather of Scotland. But whatever your state of mind, you must pack and head for Pemberley at once! Hopefully, you will find me staying there!

"Yes, hopefully, with your parents' permission, there is to be another Pemberley wedding and this time it will be mine! For some incredible reason,

Sir Robert has asked me to be his wife and we travel to Derbyshire as soon as it can be arranged. You cannot believe how happy and amazed I am at my good fortune. I love him so much. But perhaps you guessed that?

"I do not feel I am nearly good enough for him, but he says he is not good enough for me! So you see, Bennetta, you must come home at once because I cannot get married without you at my side, giving me advice as to what to wear. I do believe my old grey dress will not suffice this time!"

She put down her pen and reached out to pick up a miniature she had rescued from a drawer in the desk. It was of a lady with the same startling blue eyes she had bequeathed to her oldest son, her dark hair dressed in an old-fashioned style. She was not particularly pretty but her expression was warm and kind. Catherine had known straight away who it was when she found the portrait - Lady Alicia, who had died three years after her youngest son, Richard, had been born.

"You would have been so proud of your children," Catherine whispered. "Especially Robert. And how much you would have loved Matilda. I promise you, I will do everything in my power to love and care for them. You have my word."

High above her in the castle, Lady Honoria was also writing a letter. Her hands were painful this morning and the ink tended to splatter where she pushed too hard on the paper, but she was determined to finish the missive.

She was smiling - seeing two people so much in love had reminded her of her own husband, of the scandal of their marriage but how happy she had been. Her elderly maid found it quite alarming; she couldn't remember the last time she had seen her mistress smile.

"......and so Fitzwilliam, if my health allows, I will have the pleasure of seeing you at another wedding. I shall travel down to Pemberley with Matilda nearer the date when it is arranged. I imagine it will be the last one from the Courtney family; I cannot see Martin ever finding a woman who would care enough for him to overlook his many faults and poor Susannah is obviously destined to remain a spinster. Well, she will always have a home

with one of her brothers. They love her, which is all any of us want in this life.

"I like Miss Catherine Collins - she has courage and that will be needed if Courtney is to prosper. I intend to leave her my rubies, except for one ring which I want your daughter, Bennetta to have. She makes me smile. An amazing child. Although I fear you do not truly appreciate her. Well, well, we will talk of this when I see you.

"I am pleased for Robert, that he has found happiness at last: he is a good man, although too proud, like yourself. You had the sense to marry Elizabeth Bennet and Robert has at long last realised that it is what lies in a person's heart that is important, not what she looks like or how much money she brings to the alliance...."

Days later, miles away in Derbyshire, Elizabeth Darcy was seated at her own writing-desk. From her window she could see the great gardens of Pemberley shining in the summer sun. She could hear her daughter, Jane singing as she cut roses just outside and in the distance, she could hear shouts and laughter and knew her two boys and her husband were making their way back to the house, soaking wet - they had been swimming in the lake. Everything in her world, except for the poor health of her dear sister, brought her pleasure and deep thankfulness.

She bent her dark head to her letter.....

"It seems so odd that it will be months before this letter reaches you, dear Mary, if it ever does. I always fear the ship will sink. By then Catherine Collins will have become Lady Courtney! As you can imagine, our mama is very vexed by this as although all her daughters are married, none of us has a title!

"But I am delighted for poor dear Charlotte's sake. How proud and happy she would have been to see this come to pass for her Catherine. How it would have delighted Sir William and Lady Lucas, how they would have annoyed Mama by continually mentioning Catherine's higher title!"

"I know I can ask you to pray for the happy couple but how very far away this must all seem from your home and life in Africa. How is Matthew? I trust he has not taken a fever again this year as he did last. Fitzwilliam believes he works too hard. And your Miriam? In your last letter you said she was proving difficult. She must be seventeen by now. It seems so strange that none of us have ever seen her. What sort of life does she lead? I see her in my mind's eye much like you were yourself at that age, bookish and musical...."

In Northumberland, dusk was falling, the sun had vanished behind the hills and the ocean lay flat and calm, innocent, as if it could never cause harm and destruction. A couple strolled along the grassy peninsula towards the sea, two great dogs at their heels.

Sir Robert gazed down lovingly at the bright brown head that just reached his shoulder. "So, my Catherine, tomorrow we are for Pemberley!"

"It seems like some wonderful dream," came the soft reply. "I fear I will awake and find myself back in Longbourn, with Harriet shouting for me to come and dress her."

"If it is a dream, then it is one we share." He turned them round to stare back at the bulk of Courtney Castle, dark against the violet evening sky. "Soon this will be our home together. We will build a good life here, Catherine, I know we will."

A mischievous light gleamed in her eyes. Sometimes Robert could get too solemn. She stretched out a bare foot from under the edge of her dress. "I am afraid you may have proposed under false pretenses. I am supposed to be a girl whose main attribute is common-sense, but you see, I still have the bad habit of walking on the grass without shoes."

"A disgraceful habit, indeed. You were barefoot when I first met you."

"And when did you first decide I was to be the next Lady Courtney? I'm sure it wasn't when you thought I was a maid at Pemberley!"

Robert frowned and then smiled. "Oh, I think my heart knew the second you confronted me in the stable yard, with a yellow chick in your hands and straw decorating your hair! My head just took a little longer to catch up."

Catherine tightened her grip on his arm. "I knew the second I slid down the spiral stairway and you shouted at poor Martin when he caught me."

"I was just trying to protect you from my brother's unwanted attentions, although I admit I was a little jealous that you seemed so at ease with him. My life was so bleak, so dark, so deeply unhappy until you arrived at Courtney. You brought the light, Catherine. My fairy girl."

She sighed. "We must go in. Matilda will be wanting us to say good-night to her. She will miss us until she comes to Pemberley for the wedding."

Sir Robert nodded, then smiled. "But after that we will be together, here, forever. Come, it grows dark and the grass grows wet with dew! Mrs Crawford will have dinner waiting for us." And he swept her up into his arms and carried her back to the castle and their future happiness.

The End

COMING SOON

MIRIAM - THE COUSINS OF PEMBERLEY: BOOK 3

Miriam - stubborn, quick-tempered and impulsive has grown up disliking all she has heard from Mary, her mother, about her four aunts. Now she must leave Africa and travel to England to meet them. How can this adventurous girl with her desire for freedom possibly fit into their well-ordered world?

Coming August 15th 2022

Printed in Great Britain
by Amazon

78377506R10127